Fire in the Ice

by
Katlyn Stewart

PublishAmerica
Baltimore

First printing

ISBN: 1-4137-3278-X
PUBLISHED BY PUBLISHAMERICA, LLLP
www.publishamerica.com
Baltimore

Printed in the United States of America

Dedication

Originally, when I penned the manuscript for *Fire in the Ice*, I wrote a very simple dedication for it. A few refined words for my friends, family and husband.

However, just after finishing the book, and getting it ready to go to the publisher, my life took a different turn due to a series of events. For that reason, this dedication will be a bit longer.

First and foremost, I want to thank my husband, the backbone of my writing. Not only does he encourage me, but at times realizes that he is on the back burner while I am in "write" mode. I appreciate his strength and his undying love. I also want to thank him for the stories regarding his childhood and of his father, as they are the strength of characters for this book, as well as watching the interactions between my daughter and her husband.

I want to acknowledge my wonderful friends, my beautiful daughters, the precious gift of my grandchildren, and the much-loved family unit I have been blessed with. I could not do any of this without their understanding.

Finally, to my oldest daughter, we mourn your passing with each day of our lives; we each lost huge pieces of our hearts when you left. So because of all that you were, your life, love and contribution to society will never be forgotten.

Chapter 1

Deedra thought her life to be perfect. She was married for years to a highly respected gentleman in the community, and the affluent owner of an upscale restaurant named Fireside Inn. He had taken care of every essential aspect of her life, giving her two beautiful daughters and an exquisite home in the posh bay-front area of Sarasota, Florida.

Then without warning, that world had come crashing to the ground. Craig Marlan, the man that sheltered her against all sorrow, was killed in a car accident, a fact that would alter her faith in "Happily ever after."

Deedra was not satisfied with simply being the owner of the stylish restaurant, desperately needing to feel useful and fill the void left in her life. Craig had made it quite clear shortly after their marriage that she should stop working at the restaurant. Her life should be in her home, taking care of the "wifely" duties that a household demanded and await the birth of children. He also felt that her responsibilities should include charitable events and social activities. That his wife, a woman of means, should not be involved in such trivial things as outside employment. She did as he wished.

However, the hollowness of life without a man to care for, along with the loneliness of the huge home, forced Deedra to alter what Craig had commanded of her. Deedra decided to return to the restaurant, taking over her late husband's position, and occasionally filling in as a hostess as well. The work made her feel worthwhile, like it did in the younger days of her life. Consequently, being at the restaurant allowed her the opportunity to interact with people and keep the loneliness at bay.

Her dearest friend from youth, Marcy, also worked at the Fireside, starting just days before each other. A little over a year after Craig's death, Marcy started trying unsuccessfully numerous times to set Deedra up on dates. Regrettably, it had been to no avail. She hated watching from the sideline as Deedra put her whole life into work and children, allowing for no personal life whatsoever. As the time ticked away, everyone could see Deedra slowly slip away into her cold detached world.

Marcy was fearful that her dearest friend would never allow her heart to open, nor allow anyone to love her again. "Go out!" Marcy would say to her. "Do something besides work and go home. Maybe have a drink now and again, get a little tipsy, and laugh." However, no amount of coaxing would budge Deedra. Still, her friend hated seeing how closed off Deedra had become. She was still a young woman with so much life left to live. Marcy held on to the hope that one day, someday, someone would have the capability to break through the ice formed around Deedra's somber heart.

Her still-youthful figure, though hidden under an unflattering waitress uniform, was a joy for the male patrons of the establishment to admire. They could envision the supple roundness of her breasts and hips. Nevertheless, to their disappointment she would turn each of the potential suitors down.

Several men, over the last two years, tried using their best tactics to become a suitor for Deedra. Her captivating eyes would mesmerize them. The soft flowing movement of her body hypnotized them. But, alas, Deedra would have no part in it.

Over time, the patrons and employees affectionately began calling Deedra "The Ice Princess." A bit of a side-bar joke spoken softly when she was unable to hear. One male patron would warn another male, "She's off limits, she's The Ice Princess, no one can break through her shield."

During the loll between lunch and dinner, Deedra placed a call to the children's sitter, Mrs. Baker, to check up on the girls. All was well, as she always knew it would be. Mrs. Holly Baker, "Grandma" to Deedra's girls, had been their nanny for over six years, and a true "God send" after Craig's death. The children thought of her as their real grandmother. With Craig's parents never taking an interest in the children, and living abroad, Mrs. Baker became their surrogate grandmother and enjoyed the time spent with the children. Especially since her own children were grown and living lives of their own apart from their mother. Mrs. Baker relished in feeling useful again with the responsibilities of caring for Deedra's young daughters.

Like clockwork, Monday through Friday she was there taking care of any necessary chores Deedra could not get to and looking after the children until she came home. This allowed Deedra the freedom to handle both the business and financial side of her life.

With the phone call finished, Deedra walked to the kitchen, stopping to sample the ribs that were so famous to the restaurant. Basically, she was muddling around the Inn to find something to clean to pass the time away. Today would be another slow one. Tourist season was at a halt, with spring in full bloom. During these sluggishly hot summer months, most of the customers that came in were the old regulars that lived in the surrounding area, with the busiest period being on Friday and Saturday nights..

Stopping near the grill, Deedra shared a joke with the head cook, Mark, and was still smiling to herself as she walked back to the front. Out of the corner of her eye, Deedra saw the door open, and then heard the chimes ring, signaling to her that a customer had come in.

Back to work, finally! Making a brief stop to check her appearance in the mirror, with a quick smoothing to the uniform and checking to be sure her make-up still looked fresh, she hurried toward the front counter to greet the awaiting patron.

At first, she did not pay much attention to the man standing there waiting for someone to seat him. When she did look in his direction, the exact moment her eyes met with this stranger's, a shiver came over her entire spine, her face was instantly hot. This was no ordinary man. Indeed, he was something that one would see on a *G.Q.* magazine. Without realizing it, she was studying him head to toe.

7

Had she seen him somewhere before? Perhaps met him? *No, No,* she thought, unable to place him or his face.

Standing before her was this extremely well-built man, she guessed him to be somewhere around 6'5-6'6 or so. The largest frame on a man she had ever seen. He dwarfed her small frame from where he stood. Without consciously meaning to, her eyes followed the chiseled powerfully built definitions of his arms. They seemed to ooze out from his tight black t-shirt. Her eyes wandered from the shirt to the way the faded blue jeans fit his body as though they were made of liquid. Her mind's eye could almost imagine the hard edges of his thighs.

Allowing her eyes to move back up the wide dimensions of this man, she focused in on the deeply bronzed skin and well-weathered face, only adding to the allure of this stranger.

The hair, the gorgeous full mane of long, black silky hair, with a white cowboy hat, was a marked distinction to his deeply tanned face. This only added to the extraordinary beauty of this man. Deedra's mind continued wandering with no concept of time or the fact that he might be watching her. She explored the strong points of his appearance. The solid curve of his jaw line. The way his long hair lay to either side of his well-developed neck. The broad shoulders. He was a like a dream, a beautifully built specimen.

Even more so than this, Deedra was taken by complete surprise that her skin felt like little needles pricking away at her skin. Her heart was beating wildly, as though she were a young schoolgirl seeing a famous rock star for the first time.

Deedra tried quickly to regain her composure, unaware of how long she had been standing there staring at this man. Secretly she was praying he had not noticed her stare. Taking in a deep slow breath, she walked closer to the man.

"Good afternoon, sir! Could I see you to a table or a booth?" she asked nervously, realizing her voice was cracking. Her mouth was as dry as if cotton were in it. *What is wrong with me?* she wondered, clearing her throat so that it seemed as if she had a bit of a cold.

His reply caught her off guard even more than she already was.

"You sure can, darlin', make it a booth—for two!" He smiled, his voice deep, husky, with a distinctive slow southern drawl. A flirty smile pursed across his large expressive lips.

"Will someone be joining you, sir?" she asked innocently, her voice still not up to par.

"No, lil lady, just you!" he replied.

If he had not made her nervous enough before, she was literally shaking now, being putting on the spot this way. In her silent words to herself, she decided the best way to handle this awkward situation was to pretend she did not hear him. Besides, at this moment, words seemed to be eluding her anyway.

"Right this way!" she said, using her best manager-trained voice. Deedra turned to walk in front of him, leading him down the middle of the aisle, guiding him between the tables on either side of them. As soon as they reached the booth she was to sit him at, she stepped to the side and laid the menu down on the booth's Oak wood tabletop. Rapidly, as though in a hurry, Deedra went into the spew of information about his waitress and the specials of the day. She wanted to leave as quickly as possible. Unfortunately, she was not able to finish before being interrupted.

"Well, honey, you never answered my question, are you gonna sit with me, or not?"

Deedra paused for a moment, taking in another deep breath. Yet again, his question caught her off guard. Feeling her face returning to red like it had been just minutes before, the only thing she could think to do was look down at the floor, staring at the dark black well-used cowboy boots, and try to find words to articulate.

Where were the comebacks she usually had with other flirting customer's? Where was her self-assuredness? Always before, she could find something quick to say to ease the situation. This sudden inability to speak her mind had her dumbfounded. After all, this was her domain, never had she shown fear of going toe to toe with anyone here. This place offered her protection.

Yet, something about this man made her overly anxious and unable to utter anything without sounding absurd. Finally, in one last attempt to muster up what little bit courage she could find, Deedra turned her face up to meet his. "Sir, can I please bring you something to drink?" she asked, jaw squared, without so much as an acknowledgment to his question.

"Yeah," he answered in a tone that sounded perturbed for not getting the answers he was looking for. *I'll have to try this again*, he thought. "How 'bout you bring me the biggest jug of tea you got, sweet, sweet tea!" He snickered to himself. "Oh, and sweeten it with your fingers, darlin'."

"Yes sir, sweet tea it is," she answered. "Your waitress's name will be Marie and she will be with you shortly." She stammered the words out swiftly, nearly running the sentences together.

She hoped that her aloofness would get the point across to him that she did not want to be bothered by someone such as himself. She expected that because of the lack of dialogue on her part, he would stop asking questions that she did not dare try to answer. What crossed her mind at this moment was the need to run. Get away. For some unknown reason, the mere sight of him made her extremely nervous in her own skin.

Nervous perhaps because she knew he was watching every movement she made, every word that formed from her lips. Now that she had been able to get his drink order and tell him about his waitress, she could quickly turn and walk away. Unfortunately, she was not getting away fast enough—she heard his voice loud and clear.

"Hey. Tell me your name, lil lady," he requested, his voice strong and loud.

For a moment she stood there, feet frozen to the floor, swallowing the hard lump in her throat. She did not have the nerve to look around the room for fear that other customers overheard and were watching her reaction.

Why can't he just leave me alone? When I didn't answer him that should have told him something. Arrogant Jerk! Why must he be so difficult?

This man should not be any different, she should be able to just flit about and walk away without feeling the least bit apprehensive. She had accomplished it a million times before. So then, why was her stomach so full of butterflies that she thought she might be sick?

"Deedra," she quickly muttered aloud to him, without turning back to tell him. She quickly walked away before he could ask anything else of her.

The stranger watched her walk away, the same devilish smirk planted across his lips, very pleased with himself that he had gotten under this woman's skin. He could tell she was intrigued the moment he entered the restaurant. She liked what she saw. He observed the flickering of her eyes as they moved over his long frame. No way to denounce the nervousness in her voice.

This woman wanted to be a challenge, she was pretending to be standoffish. He liked this new game, if she wanted to play. After all, Challenge was his middle name. It was what made him who he was. He enjoyed the idea of keeping people on their toes around him. It thrilled him to make people nervous. Especially a woman, someone as unique as this waitress was.

He had surveyed her as well. What man would not? The manner in which the black shiny fabric hugged the full supple curves of her short frame. The ringlet curls of golden strawberry blonde hair that framed her face and the wisp of curls that spiraled wildly from outside the loosely fitted bun atop her head. Hard not to notice the shapely legs barely hidden from view by sheer black stockings.

Yes, a perfect challenge, an unexpected dare. He chuckled to himself. Though he should stop thinking about her and concentrate on the menu in his hands.

Disappearing in the foreground of the kitchen, Deedra told Marie she had a customer waiting. Never had she remembered being this easily annoyed in her life, but in some way, he had gotten to her. A man she did not even know, making her this nervous and apprehensive. *Especially* someone with the ability to make it difficult for her to speak in a normal tone.

Marcy was standing near the back room taking her break when Deedra came through. Inquisitively she asked about the fine looking man that Deedra had seated. It was apparent that all the female employees had noticed him. It was hard not to. Each of the waitresses were whispering wishes about what they could do with a man like that.

In a half handed gesture as if slapping at a fly, Deedra tried brushing him off as if it had been nothing. Trying her best to make Marcy believe she really had not noticed much about him at all, she could not give her any answers.

Nevertheless, typically curious Marcy knew better and kept on with her questions anyway. Deedra remained silent and blasé.

The questions kept coming anyway, until finally Deedra spoke up. "Oh come on, Marcy, he's really nothing more than just an arrogant, self important man. Thinks he is something special!" Deedra's words sounded cold, and a bit on edge from listening to Marcy ramble. "Really nothing more!"

Instantly, the response turned the inquisitive Marcy's head. Typically, Deedra had only the nicest things to say about someone, even if she wasn't very fond of them. Her spirit had always been so easygoing, never a cross word, and seldom an angry look in her eyes. Even when something got on her nerves, or she was upset at an employee, Deedra always spoke with tact and grace. So she knew by what she had said, the aloofness of the words, Deedra did not just see him as "just some arrogant man."

The thought brought a wide smile to Marcy's face, with the realization that this man could affect her like this. She would have to see for herself, and check this man out.

Sneaking around the tables to get a good look, pretending to be cleaning, she watched the movements of this man. She inspected the long glistening hair and the well-defined muscular features. Marcy silently watched as he ate, wondering to herself if he devoured a woman the same way he devoured the barbecued rib he was holding in between his large fingers. She could hear his voice as he spoke to Marie; the bass-toned deep sexy southern drawl lured her in even more.

Huge dark eyes, Marcy guessed them to be a deep brown and wished she could get closer to see the actual color of them. It was not hard to notice that he looked rough around the edges. It only added to the sensuality of this man. The appearance of his face told her he was an outdoorsy kind of a man. No longer did she have to wonder why Deedra was acting the way she was.

Even though she was happily married, Marcy could see that sexuality oozed from his veins. It pleased Marcy that at long last someone had made Deedra's heart skip a beat, maybe even chip away a minuscule piece of ice surrounding her heart. Her friend had kept herself hidden for so long from any man, shutting down any feeling or emotional connection to them.

This man, this stranger, was exactly like the man Deedra had fantasized she would marry someday, when she was a teen. Exactly as she told Marcy, she had dreamed him to be. However, telling Deedra that, well, she would never admit to the dreams she had in her past, and only argue the point.

After all, according to Deedra, Craig supposedly was what she wanted in a man. That is what she tried to convince Marcy to believe in when Deedra and Craig started dating. Marcy just never assumed it for a moment. Craig was nothing like any of the dreams she had. Deedra did not even know what a real man was when she married Craig.

"Maybe, just maybe," Marcy considered, "Deedra is finally waking up to the possibilities that there is happiness out there for her."

Pacing the kitchen floor, Deedra pretended as if she wasn't waiting for Marcy to return from her investigation. In being so nervous and apprehensive about this gentleman, this stranger, she had one of the other waitresses take over her post. She didn't want him to see how uneasy he made her. Like it or not though, her thoughts were on this man; she hated the fact that they were.

There was no clear understanding as to why she felt like a fool when she had been near him. Nor could she comprehend why a part of her was actually waiting for her friend to return and tell her every little tidbit she had learned about him. Standing in the foreground of the kitchen, hiding like a child from a monster, she was too fearful to talk to this man, look at this man. Afraid of her own thoughts.

Oh to be home, safe in her bed at this moment. Strange feelings were in the pit of her stomach totally unanswered by her own self.

Safety is what she needed most. She pushed herself into thinking about Craig, allowing the guilt to wash over her, chastising herself for looking at another man in the first place.

Was Craig watching her? Would he think her to be childish, immature?

The period since his death seemed to have occurred like a flash of light. There was no reason to look at any other man. Her heart belonged to a man that was dead. Her own sexuality had become silent, dying like the wind. Never to return. Slowly, without realizing it, she had shut herself down. It had not been intentional at first, but in time, it became a safe sanctuary for her.

She would not allow herself to feel anything with any man. In order to do that, she allowed the pain of loss to stay clear on the front burner of her thoughts. Doing so would free her from feeling that kind of devastation again.

Marcy walked in and took her away from her thoughts, bouncing along as she walked filled with excitement. "Your stranger friend left a note with Marie," she sang. "It's on a paper napkin no less." She laughed, thinking this was straight out of their teenage years.

"I told her I would bring it to you," she said, extending her hand out with the little note in it, smiling from ear to ear, a gleam in her eyes. "Open it, come on, open it, I'm dying to know what it says!" Marcy urged her friend.

Deedra took the note from her hand and smiled shyly. On the outside of the folded napkin was "Hello" written in bold black lettering. Carefully, she opened the napkin up as if the contents might bite her. She could feel her hands shaking, perhaps from the earlier encounter. Deedra hated the feeling of not being in control of her surroundings.

In a slow monotone voice, she started reading the note aloud, as if she really did not care if she read it or not.

My name is Josh. You have beautiful eyes. I didn't see a ring so you must be single. Call me. 555-1411 Anytime, Josh.

Standing there blank faced for a moment, the silence filled the air around her. Marcy watched as she rolled the napkin into a ball and

14

handed it back to her, who of course opened it up again and read it to herself.

Deedra did not dare allow Marcy to know that her stomach was doing flip-flops. That her heart was pounding so loudly she could hear it in her ears. Instead, she kept up the pretense that the note meant nothing to her at all. Marcy walked over to where Deedra was standing, studying her face intently for a few moments. Trying to figure her out. Deedra would not look at her.

A man had paid attention to Deedra; she had hoped there would be a little gleam in her eye or a smile to her face. Something.

"Dee, what's wrong? It's a cute little note, isn't it? I mean, he wants to go out with you, don't you think that's kind of cute?"

"It's just a note, so calm down!" Deedra replied.

"Yea, but, doesn't it flatter you in the least that he wrote this?" Marcy inquired of her friend.

"OK, so it's nice! That's what you want to hear, I just don't see the big deal!" Deedra sounded snippy and yet almost emotional as she spoke. "Didn't you see him? All sure of himself, thinks he's all that! Just assumes that this note will make me call him, as if I have nothing better to do. Like I would want anything to do with something like him! Who does he think he is anyway?"

Marcy started to speak; she was feeling a bit shocked at the way Deedra was talking to her, not believing this could be the same sweet girl she knew, and trying to understand why Deedra was acting this way. However, Deedra cut her off before she could form the words.

"Look, I'm going home, I am really tired! Besides, we aren't busy anyway."

"Well now wait a minute!" Marcy interrupted, but was cut off again quickly.

"I will see you tomorrow, Marcy!" she replied sharply, almost angrily, not waiting for Marcy to verbalize what she wanted to say.

Deedra exited the kitchen in a matter of seconds, not even allowing Marcy to say good-bye. Her friend just stood there stunned.

Chapter 2

Angrily, Deedra got in her car, arguing to herself about how childish this was. *Passing a note to a girl as if he were a schoolboy! How silly is that? What would give him the slightest inclination I would be the least bit interested?*

Driving home, amidst the anger, she forced her thoughts to go back to the days gone by. There was solace in forcing herself to reminisce about Craig and the past. She kept the culpability close to her heart, like a shield she wore as protective armor.

Deedra had known her place next to Craig. It was so much easier then. No responsibilities, no stress in her life. Craig was the master of taking care of everything that involved their lives.

That critical night, when the police knocked on her door, all the security Craig had given shattered like glass to the floor. Her husband was dead. A drunk driver had run a stop light, hitting the driver's door, and ended his life within a split second of time.

At first, Deedra begged for the world to stop turning, unsure of herself as to what the right steps to take were or how to cope with the devastating loss, the changes to her life, or the repercussions that came with his death.

Craig was the core of their marriage, had made all of the major decisions. He dominated their lives, even in the most diminutive details, keeping the family unit safe and secure. Keeping her safe and secure from the influences of the outside world. Suddenly, he was no longer there to tell her what was best for her and her children.

Two years, two long years, trying to gain courage and strength where none had existed. Learning to make difficult decisions. Living with the pain of a large empty house that once had companionship in it, where she knew her rightful place.

Without so much as a true grieving period, Deedra thrust herself into his businesses, trying her best to learn what she could to continue the company and the stock holdings he owned. Yet, at the same time, she tried to cling to her daughters and focus all her attention on their lives. As the stress of the new life surrounded hers, all her inner emotions slowly died.

The Fireside Inn would become her pride. It had, after all, been a part of her life from the time she was a young girl. Still in school and barely sixteen, she started work there as the part-time waitress, working the evening shift.

A year later and after her graduation from high school, the new owner Craig Marlan had taken over and renamed the large restaurant. He had the restaurant remodeled and arranged it to be a little different, with a flair of upper class style to it, yet keeping the mainstay of the old country style restaurant it had replaced, keeping the favorite dish, the smoked and deeply lathered with honey sweet barbecue sauce, pork ribs.

The Fireside would bring the downtown country charm of yesterday into the mainstream of high class of today, adding to its menu the taste of red salmon with lemon, dill and pepper sauce and the tender chicken breast with creamy mozzarella cheese and bacon as second and third in line favorites.

Craig was so much older and more mature, falling hard for the sweet, innocent Deedra almost immediately. He saw in her a childlike beauty—small-framed with strawberry-blonde long curly hair and the most captivating deep green eyes he had ever seen.

Although he knew she was young and innocent, it did not seem to dissuade him at all. After all, Craig was born into money, and for all of his life was able to have whatever his heart fancied. His heart fancied this innocent girl. Her face, body, and movements would be all he could focus his thoughts on. He had to have this child/woman for his own. In addition, he knew he could mold her into what he wanted out of a woman, a woman of style and beauty. Make the insecure child flower under his watchful eye.

Deedra never felt as though she quite fit in to anything in her life, especially in school. The family unit had come to Florida from Georgia, bringing with them their deep southern drawl, when Deedra was just a year old. Florida offered them more than what they could accomplish in Georgia, but in the end, Deedra's father worked hard for the ranches around the area as a day-labor cowboy. Even with all his hard work, the family still had a rough time making ends meet.

She cursed that life from the time she was a young teen, hated seeing her father, Sam Montgomery, work so hard, never having a life outside of his job. Never finding the time to enjoy what living had to offer. Tired and worn he would come home with never enough time for his wife and children.

Her mother Beatrice, the typical homemaker with all the chores of running a house, always made sure everything was perfect for her husband when he came home each night. She would keep the children quiet, not allowing them to inconvenience their father, never permitting any time for herself. The children—Mark the oldest and Leslie the sister next in line and Deedra the youngest— helped their mother as much as they possibly could in between their own schoolwork and friends. Mark took care of most of the outside duties, with the two sisters doing what they could to help their mother.

When Deedra reached high school, the closest school was in the city. She was thrust in a new school with other teens whose parents were more well to do. They would taunt her for her southern accent and make fun of her clothing. So, in order to fit in better, she made the decision to take extra classes in English Literature, learning to speak correctly and with more sophistication.

Once she had found the job at the Fireside, she slowly replaced her western style of clothing with neatly polished pants and soft simple dresses. She left the blue jeans and boots behind as though they were never a part of her life. So ashamed of the real life she really had, she would dress with elegance, speak with eloquence and pretend the country life she really lived did not exist.

Unfortunately, two weeks past her eighteenth birthday, both of her parents were killed in a car accident on a major highway, heading to visit relatives in Alabama. Her parents' deaths would be the beginning of the inner guilt for shunning her parents' way of life. As if in a state of shock, she lived as if stuck in a nightmarish dream that employed her continuously. Deedra found herself falling in to a deep dark depression and self-detestation. It would be the foundation for which she would build the shield of protection around herself.

Though the funerals for her parents should have brought the siblings closer together, with Deedra it did not. Mark had moved to North Florida as soon as he turned eighteen. He had his family and business there. Leslie had married at seventeen and moved with her husband back to his native town in Georgia. With the funeral over, the house and property put on the market and their parents' possessions disbursed, Mark and Leslie went back to their everyday lives. Deedra would be left alone in the small apartment she rented in town with the money received from the estate. All the dreams of a future filled with college and becoming a lawyer slowly drifted out of reach.

Thinking back to her youth only brought back the painful memories, a childhood lived as though every day was a new hurdle to jump. She was always overcoming difficulties. She had been through so much pain and instabilities in her young life.

Craig used the advantage that Deedra was alone and scared. He watched as the loneliness slowly began shutting her down. He waited patiently like a lion in wait until he knew she was ripe for the picking.

Marcy tried her best to help Deedra, even though she was too immature yet to understand the changes taking place in Deedra's personality. She tried her best to warn Deedra, but to no avail.

When Craig and Deedra began dating, the employees at the inn just could not imagine what she could see in this stoic man. After all, he was twenty years older and far more reserved than the sweet eighteen-year-old Deedra.

Coming from wealth, Craig used a great deal of money to play the stock markets and invest in high-yield bonds, which helped to make him independently wealthy aside from his family. The Fireside was just a toy he bought to give him something to do.

Of course, he looked the part as having come from money. He had a tall, thin frame, and every single strand of light brown hair on his head was kept short and perfectly coifed. He dressed for success on an everyday basis in his designer suits and ties.

Marcy could not stand how pompous he was, always looking down his glasses when he spoke to someone, the trait she disliked most about him. However, she tried her best to endure him for her friend.

Deedra could not see what Marcy was talking about. She did not see the vindictive side of Craig. No way could she believe that she was just a trophy on his arm. To Deedra, he was a kind and tender man—extremely protective of her. Craig made good, sound decisions for her and loved her with all of his heart. He told her so. He kept the loneliness, the pain of her parent's death, and the separation between her siblings at bay. Craig filled the empty spaces.

With all the long talks they had as teens, Marcy and Deedra had shared many deep dark secrets. The fantasies, the men they would one day marry. Craig was definitely not the man in Deedra's dreams. That fantasy man was passionate, strong, determined and powerful. He would whisk her away on his white horse and make passionately hot love to her, take her and make her his own.

Nevertheless, whatever the reasonings and against continuing to argue pointlessly with her about Craig, the virginal, innocent Deedra married the sophisticated, calculating and wealthy Craig.

Throughout the years with Craig, Deedra had reflected on the marriage. In many ways, it was so common, like a pair of favorite shoes. At times, it was beyond boring, with no lively conversation, no fiery passion. Not that she really missed something she had never really had, but it was not what she envisioned marriage would be. Certainly nothing like the romance novels she read in the evenings when Craig was away on business. No, none of it was Craig's style.

He was too cut and dried for such trivial matters of the heart. His life focused on appointments and calculations, nothing as impulsive as spontaneity. Even the act of sex was clean, quick and void of imagination.

Nevertheless, even with his lack of enthusiasm, he still had wonderful qualities that Deedra admired. He was highly intelligent, loyal and kind. Craig provided her with all she could ever ask or want for and was a superb father to their two daughters, Jessica and Casey.

Her daughters were each so unique, so different. She and Craig had been married less than three months when she found she was expecting. Jessica, now 10, was so self-assured and perfectly poised like her father, but with a slight flair to be adventurous, while little Casey at seven was a bundle of joy. Everything in life excited Casey, every new adventure was a dramatic event.

Their father's death had been a hard blow on the two young girls; there had been nightmares and school problems and temper tantrums to deal with during the first few months after his death. Many times Deedra wasn't sure she would be able to handle or survive through this. But thankfully, with the help of Marcy, she did get through the difficult time. Moreover, as time usually does, the healing began for the children, and with each day, they all grew stronger in their abilities to deal with what had occurred.

Deedra became stronger as a businesswoman as well, learning to cope with accountants and the pressures that go along with owning a business, and having to deal with money markets, CDs and bonds, having had no idea of the wealth her husband possessed.

Chapter 3

Josh never found the time to pursue much of anything other than work these days. It was his focus in life. It was his calling, his history, part of a family tradition that spanned three generations of ranching in the eastern county of Sarasota. The company, McKenzie Ranch, raised and sold livestock, mostly cattle for beef. But, it also had an income from the orange trees and hay it produced.

This was his grandfather's beginning.

He wanted more out of life than what was obtainable to him in North Carolina's Cherokee reservation. He took his name, Shadow Buckskin McKenzie, his family's honor and the knowledge his father had shown him regarding the raising of cattle. He bid his family a farewell, embarking on the journey to Florida to make something out of his life, more than just the son of a Cherokee.

Shadow immediately started homesteading some of the property in the desolate areas of the eastern county, slowly building his cattle ranch. Each year he would sell off some of the calves born in the spring and sell animal hides in order to buy up the remaining choice property nestled in the surrounding areas for a song. When the grandfather passed away, he left everything he owned to his only child, Josh's father, Tyler Buck McKenzie.

Josh's father worked long and hard to give his sons Deacon and Joshua the ranch for the future: it had been Buck's (as most people called him) pride and joy. He built the ranch up into one of the largest ranches in the area. Utilizing every inch of the Ranch, he was careful with what he bought and how he sold.

He worked his boys into the business when they were very little, so it was like second nature to them all of their lives. When their father passed away ten years earlier, there was not anything the two men could not handle. There had been many times Josh wished his father was still with him. Not so much for the business, as Josh knew that like the back of his hand, but for his personal life. His dad's wisdom had gotten him over many a rough spot. Though Josh was overconfidant about many aspects of his life, he still wished for the guidance and wisdom his father had possessed.

Deacon was one of the true thorns in his life. They could run the business together with no problems, but they were as different as night and day. Deacon liked getting under his skin and creating conflict between them. Both men had been known to knock heads over the most unimportant issues, then shake hands and walk away from the fight as if it had never happened. He loved his brother, but a small part of him hated Deacon, as well. Everything was always so easy for him.

His other downfall was women; his personality scared them away before he had the chance to show what kind of man he really was. He was a master at flirting, and well-educated in how to make a woman come alive in bed. He was a dangerous man when it came to a woman in his life, more apt to having a one-night stand than a long-term relationship. Sexually they wanted to stay, but his domineering side was always too much to handle. Occasionally, he would find a woman he wanted to pursue, but his die-hard personality would get in the way. He was too hard, determined, edgy. Therefore, his confidence, though he would never admit it to anyone, was low at times in the area of women.

Truly, he felt most were users, only after money, and bent on tearing away at a man's soul. Josh's one marriage in his thirty years of life had lasted a mere four years and produced two sons, Dusty and Darrin. For the boys, he was grateful, for the marriage to Lindsey Reed, he was not. It had left him with a disgustingly bitter taste in his mouth regarding the softer sex.

She had been a user, wanting money, and married Josh to get access to it. The marriage produced two sons, which she proceeded to use as her ticket off the ranch and back to the fast-paced city life she adored. With the divorce, she had gotten exactly what she wanted. Lindsey ended up receiving thirty percent of the company's earnings over the four years of marriage, payable in one lump sum, alimony until she married again, and a hefty amount of child support. The ranch house Josh had built, valued at over $250,000 could not be sold due to the fact it was part of the ranch's property. Therefore, the house was appraised and Lindsey had gotten half of what the house itself was worth, also in one lump sum.

Sometimes he hated Lindsey, hated all women. Other times he would reach out for a woman to hold, find her, only to let them go. He knew he was hard, knew he came off too strong most of the time, and that his personality was unyielding, but it was who he was. He couldn't change it.

The only woman in his life that had never let him down was his mother, Katy. She was a fiery bit of a woman whose home also sat on the eastern corner of the two hundred thousand acre plus ranch. Momma, as he affectionately called her, insisted that there was a good woman out there somewhere for Josh. He just had to have patience.

He always hugged her, made her think that he believed her words would come true. Though in the silence of the long nights, there were times he wondered if it would ever happen. He thought he had it once, and it had burned him to the bone. A happy family, like he had growing up, and like Deacon had now, he just didn't see it ever coming true.

Tonight though, lying in his bed waiting for the sleep to take him, his mind went back to the restaurant, to that woman. The short little blonde-haired woman that wouldn't give him the time of day. He reflected to himself that she was a real knockout. Not perfect, but fresh looking with large, sexy green eyes and a shapely body to match. Her hair was as golden as the sun and her lips were light burgundy-hued, pouty and expressive.

Even though she was a tiny little thing, he was sure she could hold her own if she wanted. Her eyes expressed that she was passionate, sweltering and hot. The way that she had looked at him told him that she could be electrifying in bed. He wondered to himself about the note; would she ever read it, ever call? *Naw, she won't. She wasn't the least bit interested.*

He decided to visit the Fireside restaurant as often as he could. Try to get her attention. Although he didn't know what it was about her that captivated him so much. He guessed he liked the game, the challenge. Behind those volcanic eyes and long eyelashes lay a woman. A real woman. He wanted to know everything he could about her. He could feel that she was just waiting for the creature within her to be released by a good man. Josh McKenzie figured he was just the man to do it.

He could feel the growing bulge between his thighs while reflecting about her. It excited him to think about her luscious body. How he would hold the curly hair in his fingers, hold it tightly and softly bite at her neck. Taking her like an animal. He fantasized about all the things he could do to her, if only he were given the chance. Her skin would crawl, her body would be alive with a burning desire. Just the thought made his body ache. Tonight, deep in the fantasy of her, he would relieve the throbbing alone.

Chapter 4

With the children finally off to bed, it was a perfect time for a long hot bath. The tub was filled to the brim with the sweet scent of gardenia bubble bath. She loved that smell, it was so rich and inviting. It seemed like forever since she had cared about taking a relaxing bath such as this, always opting instead for a quick hot shower before bed. Tonight, though, she felt edgy, needed something more to relax the day away. Easing herself into the hot water, she relaxed as the large bubbles licked at her stomach and breasts. Using her hands to cup the sudsy water and pour it over slowly over her skin, the heat of the water felt delightful. The scent filled up her senses. The bath was indeed what she needed to wash the day away.

After toweling off, she put her favorite purple cotton nightgown on, let out a long drawn-out sigh, and climbed under the king-sized, pillow-soft comforter.

While waiting for slumber to claim her, the image of the stranger eased its way into her head. No matter how hard she tried, she could not seem to shake the uninvited guest. All she wanted was sleep. Unfortunately, though, her mind would not shut off the images of him. Taking in a slow deep breath, she could swear there was a haunting smell in her room. A mixture of what seemed like musk and wood filled the air around her. Closing her eyes, she saw his dark naked body standing at the foot of the bed. He was perfect. Glistening tanned skin, deep rigid muscles. The long black hair lying down the sides of his face, the tips touching his chest muscles. His large expressive brown eyes pierced through her, wanting her. She felt her skin tingle beneath the covers, felt her nipples harden, something she had not felt in a long time. They were so rigid they actually felt as though they were pulsating. Something else was coming alive as well. Carefully, as if hiding something from someone in the room, she slipped her gown up just a bit and touched her fingers to the pulsating area. The area was wet, extremely wet. This was new and a bit frightening.

Like a young girl finding her own sexuality for the first time, she slowly let her fingers move up and down along the rim of the wetness. The feeling was pleasurable. Deedra moved her thighs apart just a little and let the fingers move farther into the hot wet area.

Abruptly, she opened her eyes, begging for the thoughts to stop. Moving her hands away from herself quickly, she instantly felt filthy. *This is wrong, dirty! What could I have been thinking to do this? Touching myself, thinking of a man I barely know.*

She forced thoughts of Craig to come into her mind and pushed aside the thoughts of this stranger.

When she woke the next morning, the thoughts of what she almost did the night before were far from her mind. Quietly she eased into the kitchen, careful not to make too much noise and wake the children. It was six o'clock. Jessica and Casey would be getting up in thirty minutes for school, but in the meantime, Deedra would bathe in the silence of the morning light with her coffee and collect her thoughts for the day. She didn't need to be at the Fireside until twelve, so until that time she had many things in the home to keep her busy.

Deedra did not spend many hours with the girls during the week, but when the weekends came, she made those days just for them. There were times she felt guilty for not being with the children more; she knew she really did not need to work. She had several employees at the Fireside that could be trusted.

Nevertheless, her days needed to be filled. She needed to feel worthwhile. She hated time spent alone. It was during those lonely days when she would curse Craig for leaving her, leaving the children. Then she would hate herself for having those thoughts. It was a vicious cycle of blame. It hadn't been Craig's fault, she knew that. But, there had to be someone to blame for the coldness and ache in her heart.

Sitting at the kitchen table, watching the sun peek through her window, she let her mind wander to the note that this man Josh had sent her. Really, she had to admit to herself that it was a little flattering, It made her feel warm inside to know a man had done something like that. Get the attention, she guessed. *To have someone notice that I exist.* Yet, it bothered her that she had taken it all much too seriously. Way too severely, in fact. So much so, that she thought of him last night. She could not allow that to happen again.

Other men had flirted, and she had been able to handle them with no problem, never giving them a moment's notice. So, why did he bother her so? She didn't have that answer.

In addition, OK, yes, if truth were known, it did make her feel good. And yes, she had noticed him, even though every part of her had tried not to. It was against her moral standing to think like this. She was a widow; she would remain a widow. It was just so silly to be remembering the note at all.

No quicker did she get through the door, than she was bombarded. Marcy was waiting impatiently for her. She was inquisitive as to why Deedra had left in such a hurry, why she seemed so upset at the note. Although the same age as Deedra, Marcy was more like a mother figure to Deedra than just a friend. She knew that her dear friend hid behind the death of her husband to feel safe, and as strange as it sounded, lonely. Deedra never stated anything, but Marcy knew.

Deedra, on the other hand, had always been envious of Marcy. She had been married for years to her high school sweetheart, Brad Tomlinson. Marcy was one of the most special people she had ever known. Though a bit overweight, she had a bubbly personality and a beautiful, flawless complexion. Marcy was a true prankster as well. Her shenanigans and pranks made her even more endearing, priceless in Deedra's eyes.

Marcy finally caught up to Deedra in the storage area; she couldn't stand it any longer, her curiosity was getting the best of her. "Dee, what is going on with you?" Marcy questioned. Deedra just looked at her as if she had no idea what she was talking about.

"What? What did I do now?" Deedra asked.

"You know very well what I'm talking about! Why were you so upset yesterday?"

Deedra looked over in the direction of her friend, a blank stare across her face as though she had no idea what Marcy was talking about.

"Oh! You're making way too much of this, Marcy, I just wanted to go home. If that's what you're asking about," Deedra stated matter-of-factly while walking away.

"Hey now, just a minute!" Marcy's tone rose in pitch, stopping Deedra in her tracks before she could leave the room. "I want to know what is up with you."

"Marcy, would you please just drop it, there's nothing going on, really nothing! Look, I have a lot to do, let's talk later, OK?"

Marcy stood there for a moment in total amazement that Deedra had avoided answering her questions and had simply walked off. Marcy threw the napkins she had been holding up into the air and watched them fall to the floor.

"Darn her," she muttered. "What is up with her? Something is definitely going on with her, if not, then I would have been able to get some kind of information. Either she is hiding her feelings from me, or she just darn sure will not allow herself to be a woman and enjoy that someone notices her!" The more Marcy thought on the subject, the more annoyed she became. "Guess she's just going be a spinster the rest of her life." She was still upset that Deedra hadn't at least noticed the attention she thought she should have. Her head was running wild with imagery of what she thought Deedra should be feeling right now. *Craig has been gone two years, she drifts further into herself with each passing day.*

Marcy's mind wandered back and forth throughout the day regarding Deedra and the lack of concern over the note. Not that the note itself was a big deal, but the fact that Deedra acted like nothing ever mattered. All Deedra ever had on her mind anymore was the restaurant or the children, other than that it seemed as though life was a closed subject where she was concerned.

It unnerved Marcy to no end. This was her best friend she had to watch wallow away into a make-shift, cold, desolate world. There had to be some way to get through to Deedra and help her jump start a new life for herself. Though it wouldn't be an easy accomplishment, Marcy new something had to happen or Deedra would do nothing more than waste away.

Several times in the course of the day, she tried to have a conversation with her about the note, about the man that sent it, and even about her life. Deedra would shut her off and go to the opposite end of the restaurant, so she would not have to answer or discuss anything with Marcy.

Chapter 5

It had been a long afternoon for Deedra, She was thankful that the dinner shift was almost finished. She was tired, and her feet were achy. Going to the ladies room, she decided to take a small break and freshen her make-up for the remaining night's shift. Linda, the other hostess for the restaurant, had called in earlier, sick with the flu. Deedra called Mrs. Baker and asked if she would mind staying with the girls for the rest of the evening while she covered Linda's shift. Of course, Mrs. Baker said she would be happy to.

Applying a fresh coat of lip gloss, she remembered that she had a meeting in the morning with John Sims, her accountant. Craig had trusted John and his knowledge for years, so when he died there had never been a doubt in Deedra's mind that she would remain with him and his firm. Staying with John seemed the easiest thing to do, since she had little knowledge about financial portfolios, and she didn't have any idea who else she could trust to handle her affairs.

Coming back out to the front, with some of the waitresses still on their break, she decided now was a good time to check the cash drawer, remove all the unnecessary monies, and slip them into the envelope for the deposit in the morning before her meeting with John.

In the back of her mind, she heard the door open from the sound of the chimes at the front door, though she did not look up right away from her task at hand. When she did finally stop, she realized the "stranger" was standing only a few feet away. Without really focusing on him, she could smell the intoxicating aroma of his cologne filling the air around her. Instantaneously, her body went into overdrive; every sense awakened. Immediately, her nipples hardened beneath the bra. This definitely was a new sensation. It stopped her cold in her tracks, making her question her own body.

Not again! What is it about him? she wondered. Yet it was reacting against her will with an ache from somewhere deep within. Something about him made the fine hairs stand up on end on her arms and behind her neck.

Automatically, the nervousness returned. The lump thickened in her throat. She did not dare look up to see his eyes; Deedra could feel the stare of them burning through her skin. The man, the one behind the note, the man with the breathtaking smell. Sleek boots, tight faded jeans and a dark blue western shirt fit him snugly around the rolled-up sleeves of his arms. She knew the way his rough, worn, cowboy hat fit him perfectly, as though it were apart of him, without even looking.

Without actually drawing attention to the fact that she was looking, she snuck a quick glance. His long black hair was pulled tightly into a ponytail behind the hat. A shiver ascended her spine. Her breath quickened, and her heart began to race at the mere sight of him.

"Why didn't you call me?" Josh broke the silence between them. His voice was deep and raspy, the air of his southern drawl thick as morning fog. "I waited half the night."

Deedra took sight of herself for a moment, biting down on her lower lip. *How arrogant a man is he,* she thought. "I'm sorry, sir, but I'm not in the habit of calling strangers," Deedra answered briskly, trying her best to remain polite.

"Would you like a table?" she asked, as if he were just a customer that had entered, as if he had never asked her a question.

"How about we start with you dropping the 'sir' stuff. Sir was my daddy, and I don't think I'm an old man yet," Josh replied, a bit of a gruffness in his tone. "Would you have lost your job if you had called me?" he asked directly. He looked at her with his piercing hypnotic eyes.

Damn those eyes. Her stomach immediately did a flip, and she was positive he would be able to see how uneasy he was making her.

"Sir, excuse me, but I do have other customers," she stated coldly, her voice tense. "Can I please show you to a table?" she asked, extending her hand out toward the row of perfectly positioned tables, her finger pointing the way.

"Show me a table! Show me a table!" he answered a bit on edge, making a gesturing motion with his hand like shewing away a fly toward the cluster of tables. *Damn! I am really wasting my time with this one. This little lady isn't gonna give, not one ounce. Must be an old shrew.* Josh wasn't used to being ignored like that; most women loved his flirting, enjoyed listening to the deep southern tone of his voice. Just his looks alone would make some women seek him out for conversation and other things. They wanted to get to know him, be around him. Nearly everyone thought him to be very handsome, sexy, and oh did he know it.

He thought about trying to put the charm on one more time, break the ice with her, maybe even tell her a funny joke, then decided against it. If his charm wasn't getting her attention just yet, then he would take it a bit slower and put forth more effort in reaching her with his wit.

She may take a little bit of coaxin' to break her down. He smiled to himself, watching the way her body moved as she guided him to his table. It would not have mattered anyway trying to pursue her today; she hurriedly showed him his table, sat the menu down and quickly turned on her heels to leave. There was no announcement of who his waitress would be or what the specials of the day might be either.

Josh just smiled to himself at the orneriness of this woman. She would take a lot of work to get her in the flirting mood. But, he knew eventually he would accomplish it; after all, she was the one that looked him up and down yesterday, admiring what her eyes saw.

Looking around the large dining area, he wondered why he had never taken the time to come in here before. Though a bit elegant for his taste, it was beautiful, and the ribs were fantastic. But, he guessed he had spent so much time at the local eateries closer to him he had never thought about this place when he had the opportunity to venture this far into town. After all, this wasn't the plain old burger-and-beer joints he liked to hang out in when he would decide to come in to town.

Deedra was glad to get to the back of the restaurant; her legs felt like jelly, and she would be damned if she would let him see that for some reason he had a way of getting under her skin and annoying her. He was intriguing, though, and she realized that it was best to stay away from a man like him. There was just something…wicked about him.

Just an arrogant, self-serving man! Condescending! Thinks he's God's gift or something.

Going back to finishing the task he had interrupted, she knew without even looking that he was watching her every movement. He was there playing with her mind, making her uneasy, with every customer she spoke or laughed with.

Yet, there was a thrill to it as well, though she hated to have to admit it. Slightly sinful possibly, because she knew it was driving him crazy that she wasn't flirting with him. Perhaps because she knew she had something he could never possess. *Hmmmm,* she contemplated, *what can it hurt for him to watch?*

It was foolishness to have thoughts such as this. It was a bit embarrassing on her part that when she walked through the room she did so with more elegance and sensuality. She must be absolutely crazy for behaving in this manner. There was nothing ladylike in drawing a man's attention, with no plans of ever backing it up.

In any case , he was the one that was showing interest in her, she hadn't done anything. She had tried to be blunt with him, not answer his questions. She had been standoffish. Yet, even with the coldness, he had written the note, and he had come back here, continuing the charade. So, why not let him see something that he would be forbidden to have?

Chapter 6

For over four months, Josh frequented the restaurant often. Over the period of time, he had rubbed off on Deedra just a little. Though she still would not allow for anything more than casual conversation, a small part of her was playing his game as well. Once in a while she would flirt just a bit with him, but nothing more. Perhaps her walk was a bit pronounced, maybe she leaned over more than she should. But, Deedra still believed that it was harmless and a full payback for the fact that he would not leave her alone.

He barely knew anything about her, yet she intrigued him. What he had learned was through conversations with Marcy or one of the other employees. Though somewhat tightlipped, they did let him in on the secret name for her: "Ice Princess." He believed it was a perfectly fitting name for someone so closed off and reserved.

On occasion, when curiosity would get the better of Deedra, she would break down and ask Marcy small details of the conversations that went on between them. Marcy would feed her little tidbits about the man, but just enough to keep her wanting more. It was like a game of cat and mouse, Deedra showing a tiny amount of interest, albeit limited at best, but not willing to admit it to even Marcy that there was some interest in him. Instead, Deedra would act nonchalant when given the information she requested.

So Marcy figured that if Deedra was going to play this hard to get, then "three" could play this game, with Marcy having a bit of fun at playing the game as well.

At first, he thought she was just a snippety broad, thinking she was better than anyone else. But over time, watching her, there were times he thought better of it.

Between the light conversations with Marcy about her friend, and Josh watching her movements, he thought perhaps she really did not know how to flirt. Maybe she was guarded as well, reticent. Her facade was to pretend to be snobbish so that she could protect herself.

Whatever the reasoning, he still felt the woman was a challenge. He decidedly made promises to himself that for now he was not giving up. All walls were made to be broken through, including Deedra's. It became a kick for him to frequent the Fireside at least twice a week and learn Deedra's schedule of work down to a science.

At least she had started greeting him by his first name. He in turn would make her cringe a little every time he called her his new nickname for her: "Sunshine." Especially when he would do it in front of other patrons. Particularly when he would add that sweet sexy smile of his to go with it.

Like a schoolboy with his fist crush, he remembered the month he met her—May. This was now August. The woman he was so sure he would have charmed by now was not charmed at all. In actuality, she was more like a thorn in his side, and he was not really sure she was worth the time. Nevertheless, there was something magnetic about her that could not be explained. He seemed to like her hard edges, her strengths. Her coyness.

Something in her eyes drew him in, a sound in her voice when she was not even speaking. Though she seemed to have so many fears and apprehensions, she walked with ease and presence. Her flirting was awkward, yet there was an air of untapped sexuality about her. Josh felt the overwhelming need to tap in and taste the sweet nectar that was Deedra. Therefore, even if he wanted, he could not seem to forget her and stop coming to the restaurant.

She dominated his dreams deep in the night; his mind and body fixated on her. He would conjure up the most powerful of fantasies with her as his star. She would come to him in the still of the darkness, give herself to him willingly. She was always amazing.

The most enchanting of apparitions. He would take her repeatedly in his fantasy of her. Make her want more. Scream out for more of him. There was a fire inside the pit of her being that only he would have that ability to quench. Then deep in the hour of darkness he would release the pent-up frustrations, make the ache cease to exist—for the moment.

Nevertheless, aside from those powerful dreams of her—the most dominating of his feelings—a sensation came over him that he could not explain whenever he looked in her eyes. A feeling like nothing he had known before in his life. It was an overwhelming sense of need to protect her, as if she was calling out to him silently like a scared child in danger. Something behind those expressive eyes talked to him, urged him to go on, reach out to her.

Deedra was not as reserved as Josh thought her to be. Though she kept him at arm's length, it was not because she really wanted to. It had more to do with what she perceived her moral fiber to be. How the world should see her as a person. The fact was that she was and would always be a widow, and she needed the world to be aware of it. She wore the badge of guilt like a protective coat of arms; it gave her the feeling of safety. It was her fortification from any further pain. There had been more than enough of that in her life. More guilt than any one person could imagine. Therefore, the word "widow" offered her the safety net of never having to leave the world she had created.

If truth be known, she could not wait for him to walk into the Fireside. To look into his eyes for a brief moment. To smell his scent. Yet, once he was there, she could not wait for him to leave either. He dominated her thoughts during the day and entered into her dream world at night. No matter how much she begged herself to stop the dreams, they would continue to preoccupy and at times overwhelm.

Before, during and even after Craig's death, she never remembered envisioning a man touching her during the night as she slept. The vision was so real that she felt his hands on her, his warm breath against her skin and even smelled the deep musky scent of a man still evident in the room after she woke. Wide awake, the dream over, he was still there filling up her senses, haunting her.

Without a doubt, she would wake from the dream to find that her body was slick with sweat and on fire. The sensitivity of her skin, the white-hot burning desire washed over her as if he were really there. She would lie there, trying to calm her breathing, willing her body to be still. She hated these feeling, cursed them. Then loved the feeling and relished in them. In the end, she would wonder if she were losing her mind.

As much as she despised it happening, since meeting Josh, Deedra would spend many nights lying in her bed begging for the phantom of Josh to come in to her room and take her. She ached for the silent apparition to touch her. Her mind knew how wrong and immoral it was to feel this way, but her body disobeyed her wishes to the point that the ache was greater than the will of her psyche. Slowly, she would move her hands—Josh's hands—across the naked flesh beneath her covers. The edge of her fingertips would explore the softness of her breast. Then gradually, she would allow the palms of her hands to move on either side of her stomach, outer and inner thighs. The fingers would meet in the middle, touching the highly sensitive inner area of the triangled mound. The area was moist, burning and agonizing with desire. Her breath would quicken, her hips would move rhythmically with that of her fingers. Her thighs would open wider, impatiently begging for the release. Swiftly the orgasmic sensation would rise up her spine and a low rumbling gasp would escape her lips.

With her body still coming down at a snail's pace from the ache, the guilt would immediately wash over her. She was filled with unbelievable shame for dreaming of another man besides her husband, and the deep humiliation for touching herself with her own hands.

Every time that she let her guard down this way, Deedra would take three steps back from her previous position with Josh. Though he didn't really understand why. Her culpability was driving a wedge between his pursuit of her and what she believed was right. Most definitely, she no longer had total control of her own emotions.

She was too embarrassed to talk to Marcy about what was happening, afraid that she would tell her to let go, allow the feelings in. Yet, she couldn't allow this. If she let her guard down in any fashion, it would only bring with it the increased chance for more disappointment and sorrow.

The only person with any sense about her, it seemed, was Marcy. She was no idiot, and she darn sure wasn't blind to the fact that she could see how the two acted around each other, could see the sparkle in Deedra's eyes though her words would speak of intolerance, self-centeredness, and boisterousness when she said anything about Josh.

She had been friends with her long enough to realize there was much more to her actions than her words. She knew that Deedra was the hold up to the relationship, so being the friend that she was, Marcy decided to take matters in her own hands. Marcy would have to help things along and become the matchmaker in this scenario....

Wednesday of the following week, and after having to talk her husband Brad into this little "date," Marcy decided to have the two star-crossed lovers over for dinner, without Deedra having any knowledge that Josh would be there. That afternoon at the Fireside, Marcy put her plan into action.

When Josh came in at his usual time, she walked over to his table and blatantly told him, not asked him, of her plan and the invite for dinner. Marcy explained that this little game had gone on long enough. She would really like to see Deedra find some happiness. Since Deedra was not going to make the first move and Josh did not seem to be pushing hard enough, then she would take matters into her own hands. He just smiled as she spoke to him as if it were a do or die kind of dinner and totally agreed with the plan. He would be there six o'clock sharp the next night.

Chapter 7

Nearing the appointed time of arrival, Marcy, her usually calm self, was becoming just a little nervous. Everything was prepared and ready to go; the kid's were all over at their grandmother's house. The countdown to the minutes would begin in Marcy's mind.

Brad was just as nervous, though not exactly for the same reasons as Marcy. He was rather shy about meeting new people, did not make friends easily, and he was not so sure that Marcy wasn't making a huge mistake.

Time would tell soon enough, he imagined. Silently he was hoping that Dee would forgive Marcy for meddling in her business.

Deedra checked her appearance in the mirror and gave the last-minute instructions to Mrs. Baker before leaving. As usual, Deedra had picked out one of her favorite dresses, a burgundy, Victorian, velour dress. She loved the way that velour and velvet felt against her skin, so soft, warm, and breathable.

Marcy answered the door to the tall gentleman standing in her doorway, immediately introducing him to her husband. There was no way not to notice what a truly handsome man he was. No way not to notice that his presence filled the room. His long black hair was tied loosely behind the black felt cowboy hat tipped forward just a bit to shadow the essence of his eyes. His deep black jeans fit snugly against his taunt thighs. The intense turquoise-colored

Western shirt fit his chest and the black suede boots with their shiny silver tips justified the entire outfit.

Marcy inspected him for an instant—a moment of silence. Then she realized she was standing there with her mouth half opened. Quickly regrouping, she explained that Deedra had not yet arrived and that, in fact, she had told her to arrive 15 minutes after his arrival to ensure she would not figure anything out.

Brad was pleasantly surprised that he immediately liked this man; he had a natural comical side to him. His stories, though true, were told in such a way that you could not help but laugh.

"You should have been a stand-up comic, you know that?" Brad quipped. Marcy smiled to herself. At least he and Brad were getting along well. That was a very good sign to her that Josh was just the type of man Deedra needed. If Brad liked him, he had to be special. Brad didn't make friends easily.

Hearing the sound of a car outside, Marcy quickly went to the door, even before Deedra had a chance to get out of her car.

"Whose truck is that?" Deedra inquired, looking over toward the large, black, four-wheel-drive diesel truck dominating the driveway.

"Just a friend I invited over, hope you won't mind," Marcy stated matter-of-factly, as if it were no big deal. "Come on into the living room and see." There was a bit of excitement in her voice.

Stepping from the foyer into the living room, Deedra could clearly see who Marcy's friend was; her eyes went wide, and a flush of red spread across her face. Anyone in the room could see that she was not at all pleased by what her friend had done.

"Well hello there, Sunshine!" Josh spoke, easing himself off the couch to greet her, cowboy hat in hand.

"Josh." She nodded her head toward him. "How are you?" She exchanged pleasantries, a bit of sarcasm in her tone. Fact was, at that moment she really did not care how he was.

"My what a coincidence it is that you and Marcy are such good friends all of a sudden, wouldn't you say?" she questioned, trying to keep her voice calm and not show the anger and embarrassment she was really feeling.

41

Deedra walked through the living room rather quickly and into the kitchen, positioning herself against the counter, and waited impatiently for Marcy to be on her heels behind her. *Of all the tricks to pull,* she thought to herself, standing against the counter next to the refrigerator, staring angrily at the floor.

Deedra gave her friend absolutely no time to speak as she came into the room. "What is going on here, Marcy? What the hell are you trying to pull?"

Oops! Marcy reflected.

"Oh, Deedra, it's just dinner! Don't be like this, please?"

Deedra just glared at her, shooting daggers with her eyes.

"Look, I just wanted you to have a little fun, I thought this would be enjoyable for you. You know?"

Her friend was trying her best to smooth over the situation. "Oh, I really appreciate it, Marcy! Really, I do." Deedra was gritting her teeth. "Really, I do!" she repeated. "But what gives you the right to decide what I want or need in my life?" She kept her voice low, trying to keep Brad and Josh from hearing her anger. God she hated having to be irate with Marcy, but this was way out of line in her eyes.

For a moment Marcy stood there in silence, trying to think of something funny or light to say that would ease the tension. For the first time, though, nothing funny was coming to mind. "Come on, Deedra, what can it hurt? Just dinner!"

Deedra cut her eyes at her friend. Both women stood in an icy silence.

"Just dinner and then I leave, Marcy!"

"OK. Just dinner, I promise! At least try to be nice to him, for me?" Marcy was begging her friend. "Just for tonight?"

"All right, all right, but I swear as soon as dinner's over, I'm out of here!"

She would put forth the effort, even though she was still not pleased with what her friend had done. As the night wore on, though, she was clearly surprised at this "country bumpkin," finding that Josh was more than she had originally imagined him to be.

He was extremely intelligent, funny, and a superb storyteller. He could add the most delightful annotations to the account. Several times she caught herself laughing out loud, then would realize what she was doing and stop only to be caught up again in his words.

She couldn't help but notice the way his muscles tightened and relaxed in his arms and neck as he told the stories. The movement of his mouth as he spoke. The huge deep brown eyes that spoke even when he wasn't. The wink of his left eye, when he made eye contact with her. He seemed so self-assured, almost as if he had been to visit many times before. He was so comfortable within himself and his surroundings.

He spoke of his sons, his love for them shining through in his eyes. She learned he wasn't much of a drinker and would rather spend an evening doing dinner and a movie or walks over that of the bar scene. Though silently he thought about the fact that he did frequent the bars to find potential "dates."

He told them he worked on a ranch outside of town and had lived in the country all of his life. Deedra was not only impressed with his knowledge but also that he was well read, finding him easy to debate a topic with as well.

Josh spent most of his time studying Deedra's features: the delicate way the burgundy dress complimented her red-blonde hair and the soft pale peach skin. He watched in delight as she twirled her ringlet curls around her fingers as she talked, the flicker of light that would sparkle in her beautiful doe-shaped green eyes when she was relating something that happened in her life. He couldn't help but watch her full, deep pink lips as they moved, allowing her words to flow out and the pretty sound of her voice as she spoke.

She was so shy and childlike in so many ways, self-conscious of every move she made, and yet, Josh didn't see her as that way at all. He noticed how small her features were in comparison to her large eyes and lips. She had passionate and smoldering eyes, a unique, yet beautiful face, and a natural sexiness to her movements.

He also could not help but notice how intelligent, warm and giving she actually was. When she laughed at a joke he told, her laugh was light and airy. There really was not anything that he did not find attractive about this woman. Yet, he knew deep down that she wanted to be anywhere in the world besides this living room with him.

Marcy, the instigator, was keeping the conversation going and taunting Deedra to tell Josh things she did not really think were any of his business. But to keep from causing a scene with her friend, she did tell him about her two young girls and about Craig and his sudden death. He could almost see the pain in her eyes as she talked openly about it.

It also made many things about her character become more crystal clear. She had lived through a painful period and was holding on to it with all that she had. He realized that it was not just him that she didn't want, it was any relationship with any man. She had guarded her heart from further pain. Therefore, it did not matter what man it was, she was not giving in so that she could feel the pain again.

However, with those realizations came the silent decision that he would do all he could to break down the walls she had built so sturdily around her.

There was one other surprise as well, one he had never imagined. Deedra was not only the hostess of the Fireside, she also owned the place.

The more Josh spoke about his life and about himself, the easier Deedra felt around him, a fact that was driving her crazy. It was a double-edged sword. What made her comfortable also made her want to retreat, withdraw and hide.

He seemed so rough and worn, high-spirited and cocky. Though he wasn't much older than she, he seemed to have lived a lifetime longer. He was street smart, aggressive and handsome to a fault. Dark and mysterious, with emotive burning eyes to match. She could not help to notice the sheen from his long dark hair and how beautifully the long straight tail lay against his back.

Before any of them had realized it, it was after two a.m. and well past time for them to leave. It was long past what Deedra originally said she would do. Deedra was the first to say she really had to be going. With so many mixed emotions going on inside of her during this dinner party, most of which she did not understand, she was very relieved that she could finally get out of there.

Josh was busy wondering to himself if she liked him or not. It was so hard to tell, hard to tell if she ever would be much more than a distant friend to him. Nevertheless, he was at least glad to have been given the chance to see her one on one and away from the restaurant.

When he told her he would walk her to her car, the lump returned to her throat immediately and the uneasiness surfaced again.

Josh was feeling his own emotions; he wanted to bend down and kiss her. No, no, he wanted to kiss her hard. Really he wanted to see the wide-open look to her eyes when he did astound her, shock her. But he knew if he tried anything like that, all he would get would be a slap to the face. This was not the time. He would have to find the right time.

She was feeling the same type of emotion mixed in with her feeling of flight. So many times she had touched him in her dreams, smelled the scent of him in her room, allowed her senses to fill up with him. She could almost taste his breath from where he was standing. Her body ached for him to touch her, hold her. Her body was turning against her.

Yet, her mind disliked everything that he was about; he was much too tall, much too built for her liking. He was too forward, too sure of himself. He spoke too loudly, he was much too boisterous. His manner of dress was old-fashioned with the way he wore the customary Levi blue jeans, Western-cut shirts and unoriginal cowboy boots. Not to mention the worn cowboy hat. *Who wore cowboy hats anymore? Probably never had a suit on in his life either.*

She had to stand firm, the dislike stronger than the like. A battle of wills went on between what the mind and body perceived him to be. She fought the inner turmoil, willing her mind to rule out everything else.

For Josh, there was nothing he didn't find attractive, nothing about her he didn't want. He could have grabbed her up in his arms at this very moment and been pleased. There was an overpowering need to make her want him. Instead, he wished her a good night and watched as she pulled out of the driveway, leaving him to wonder whether or not she had just endured him through this entire night.

Chapter 8

As with all Sundays, this was Deedra's day for sleeping in late, then lazing around the house. The children always amused themselves with their cartoons and video games. When their mother had gotten her bearings together and dressed, they would head over to the little café downtown that served breakfast twenty-four hours a day. They would share what went on in their lives during the week and relax. From there, they would spend the remaining day together doing whatever her girls decided they wanted to do.

Deedra rolled over and looked at the clock. It was eight-thirty and she was wide-awake. It felt too warm and cozy to get out from under the covers just yet. Instead, she lay there, closing her eyes and hoping that perhaps she would drift back off to sleep. Her thoughts turned to the week before, the dinner at Marcy's, then to Josh and the intensity of him.

What made such a man as himself tick? What was it about him that he somehow seemed to touch deeply a place in her she had no control over? In some ways, there was an attraction. Perhaps it was out of loneliness? Whatever it was, he seemed to have the ability to touch a part of her that had lain dormant for years, and in some odd way, had never existed.

Throughout the week he came into the Fireside especially to see her. She allowed herself the time to talk to him while he was there, light conversations only, of course. She kept herself on guard, careful not to say or do anything that would give him the impression that she was interested in him. There were too many things about him that made her uneasy. Yet, even with the uneasiness there was a small part of her that could not begin to explain the small bit of interest she did have in him. Still, he would inhabit her dreams, come into her thoughts at the most inopportune times. A part of her wanted him so badly it hurt and yet, she realized that she could never allow a relationship with him for fear of what would happen in the future. There was no future. Could never be a future. Certainly not with a man such as himself. She had spent her young life trying to displace herself from the country, so even if she were looking for a man, which she was not, Josh was not the type she would want in her life.

The knock on the front door brought her back to reality. She lay there for a moment listening, wondering who on earth would be there at this time of the morning, especially a Sunday morning.

"People should know better," she mumbled to herself, thinking that it must be Marcy come over to chat. She was curious to know, but she didn't dare walk out there and see. She didn't want to go half dressed with her hair all tousled about her head in case it was a neighbor of hers. She heard little feet running toward her room and sat up in the bed just as Jessica came barreling through the door.

Jumping onto her mother's bed with one swift leap, she said, "Mommy, some guy is here, he knows you!"

Oh no! She reasoned in her mind, immediately becoming nervous at the thought that the man was Josh.

"What's his name?" Deedra asked her out-of-breath and excited daughter, fearing the words that would come from the child's mouth.

"Uhmmm...." She thought for a moment. "Josh, I think he said. Anyway, can we go horseback riding? Pleaseeeeee?"

"Horseback riding? Are you kidding me? Neither of you girls has ever been on a horse!" Deedra answered quickly, gulping at the air in her throat at the thought of Josh standing in her house. Hurriedly she started out of the bed.

Deedra had just made it to the bathroom when her youngest, Casey, grabbed hold of her leg and started begging, "Pulleeeeeeeze, Mommyyyyyy, puleeeeeze can we go?"

47

"Casey, please stop that!" her mother urged.

"But, Mom," Casey begged.

"He says he's a friend of yours! We can have pizza and everything! Come on, can we, Mom, can we?" Jessica continued to plead her case.

Deedra was utterly floored; she didn't know what to say to them or what to do. He had already gotten the children too excited. It angered her that he had the nerve to come here unannounced and entice the children this way. "Let me speak to Mr. McKenzie first! Tell him I will be right there."

Josh was standing in the living room of the massive home. He could hear the children's persistent pleas to their mother. He smiled to himself listening to them. Looking around the surroundings, he was entirely amazed by such an exclusive upscale environment.

My Gawd, this woman is way out of my league. I have no chance with someone that is so much better than I will ever be, he rationalized to himself. But that thought alone didn't stop Josh for a moment in thinking that they could not be a good match.

Every detail of the surrounding rooms adjoining the living room were color coordinated all the way down to the carpet on the flooring and the marble tile of the foyer. After much too long a time looking over the interior, his impatience started getting the best of him, so he decided he would help the kids along with their begging.

Before Deedra could get to the bathroom to straighten her hair and throw her robe on, Jessica was announcing that "Mr. Josh" was already in the room.

"Mommy, look, here he is, talk to him now!" Jessica yelled out excitedly.

Deedra looked from out of the bathroom door to find that in fact, he was standing in her room. *Oh my Gawd, the nerve!* Instantly she felt both embarrassed and angry, trying to hide her gown the best way she could.

"Good morning, Sunshine!" He grinned widely. "I hope you don't mind my askin' the kids first!" He was looking her up and down in her small blue nightgown that left nothing to the imagination. He could see from the look on her face she was not at all thrilled by him being there. Josh chuckled to himself that he had caught her totally off guard, and he loved it!

Oh well, if he hadn't gone through the children, she would have said no to his invitation without even so much as a thought.

"I really don't think you should be in here! I will meet you in the living room, Josh, if you don't mind?!" Deedra snapped.

Smiling sheepishly at the girls, he winked at them, turned on his heels and swaggered back down the hallway, a huge smirk planted firmly on his face.

Now she might be a strong one, I tell you what! He nodded to himself.

Deedra hurriedly combed her hair, washed her face and quickly put on her robe. She was without a doubt becoming angrier the more she thought about what had just occurred. No sooner did she step into the living room than the children were all over her again about going...

She had a few things to say to Mr. McKenzie. She was going to usher the children out of the room in order to say her piece, but unfortunately, before she could Josh piped in and fed fuel to the fire.

"Look, you will like it at my house, the kids will have a ball. They can ride horses, take walks, play with my sons. What harm can it do?"

Deedra started to answer him. "Look, I appreciate—"

Josh cut off her words before she could say no. "Oh, now don't turn me down, come on, the kids want to go so badly."

"The girls can't ride horses," she announced.

"That's all right, there's still plenty to do, and I can teach them. You ride, don't you?"

"I have ridden, yes, a long time ago though," she answered, remembering for a brief moment the teenage years of her life.

"That's good enough! Come on then! No reason why you shouldn't come out."

He had the girls so energized by now that Deedra didn't know how to say no to them without hurting their feelings.

So, while gritting her teeth and letting her body signal to Josh that she was not at all thrilled about any of this, she gave in and told him she would bring them out as soon as she fed the girls.

Josh grinned to himself as he wrote the directions down on a small piece of paper that Jessica handed him, then winked again at the two young girls as he excused himself and left.

He left Deedra standing there with no options she could think of quickly enough to back out. He had used the girls against her. That really made her livid at him for doing that. What an uncomfortable position he had put her in. She would have to spend an entire afternoon at his home and try to make small talk long enough to satisfy her children so that she could get them to go home; the awkward position was not over by far.

Chapter 9

Already overanxious due to the long ride to the ranch, Josh was a bundle of nerves anticipating their arrival. His sons had been down at Deacon's house having breakfast with their cousins, giving Josh even more time to think about the fact that he had just driven all the way to town and talked Deedra and the children in wanting to come out.

Well, OK, he didn't really "talk" Deedra into anything; He essentially had talked the kids in to it, thereby getting their mother involved. He knew it was wrong to use the children this way, against their own mother's wishes, but hey, it worked! She was too contrary to have come any other way. So he had no choice but to push. He had explicit plans for the two of them today. One way or another, he would find a way to be alone with her. The ache in the pit of his belly was more than he could stand. He had made love to her repeatedly in every position in his mind. If he was unable to do anything else today, he would at least kiss her. His sons would keep the girls busy at one part of the ranch, while he would try his best to lure Deedra to the other end. Two hundred thousand acres was a darn good place to start at trying to be alone with her.

He busied himself trying to clean up the house, straightening it as best he could. He was no housekeeper; he had a woman, Mrs. George, that took care of that three times a week. But the boys had been there and messed it up a little.... Miss Deedra would just have to understand.

The drive out of town was so peaceful that her anger toward what Josh had done seemed to be subsiding. She had forgotten how beautiful this area of the county really was. Most of her adult life had been spent near the beach. There had not been any reason to drive out east of town, no reason to be in the country. Not since the death of her parents. Matter of fact, she detested the country. The smells, the long winding roads that seem to go nowhere. Nothing but acres upon acres of cattle and grassland. Though it really wasn't the country itself that she disliked, but the sad memories of a childhood gone wrong. So many "if only's." If only she hadn't wanted to get away from that life so badly, would her parent's still be alive? Would life have been different if she had accepted who she was with the clothing styles and the southern drawl she had been so ashamed of? Were her parents taken from her as a way to teach her a valuable lesson about her selfishness?

She wondered who the owners of this ranch was, would they mind people traipsing around on their property? Certainly Josh would not have asked them to come if it were not OK with the owners.

Jessica broke into the silence of Deedra's thoughts. "Where did you meet him, Mom?"

"Oh, I met him at work," she cautiously replied.

"Is he your boyfriend?" she questioned again.

"Oh no. No, he's not, just someone that I know," Deedra answered quickly.

"Well, he kind of acts like he is," Jessica exclaimed.

"Well, he's not, Jessica! Look, honey, why don't you two just sit back and enjoy the ride." She didn't want to have to answer any more questions from her girls; she was nervous enough as it was.

It had taken her nearly twenty minutes just to find something she could wear out to a ranch. With only two pairs of jeans to her name, and not having worn them in years, they fit a bit snugly at the waist. She searched for a t-shirt of some sort to wear with them, but found that all she had were the ones she used to clean in, and they were stained to the max. So, finally she found a simple, flowered, silk shirt that went to one of her other skirt sets. The only shoes that would fit anywhere near the type of footwear comfortable enough for the country was a pair of black Victorian boots with a low heel that she had bought to go with another favorite dress. This outfit would just have to do.

It seemed like they had been on the road nearly forty minutes before finally arriving at the mouth of the next road they were to take. Deedra was met with total surprise when she saw the large sign over top the road, burnt on the wood in large block letters: McKENZIE RANCH, with the smaller M BAR R insignia just below it.

In her wildest dreams, she never would have imagined that Josh worked for his own family's ranch. It never dawned on her when he said he worked on a ranch that he was speaking of his own and wasn't just a ranch hand for someone else, like her father used to be.

The hard-panned dirt road they turned off on seemed to take forever as well, with so many bends and windings along its trail. The road sign on this road said McKenzie Ranch Road. What she saw was enough to make her forget any of her prior thoughts. Acres upon acres of beautiful pastures were closed off to the rest of the world by miles and miles of dark brown wooden fencing with barbed wire fencing on the cross sections of the land.

She followed it for just a little bit before coming to another smaller road to the side that read McKenzie Lane. Driving past this road she could see homes in the distance that looked very similar to each other. She guessed them to be the true ranch hands' houses. She continued along the main road, a double wide sloth cut around large oak trees, pine trees, ponds and an even larger pond almost the size of a small lake. Passing by another small dirt road, she saw another wood sign similar to that of the original at the mouth of the main road, also in huge lettering: BUCK'S PLACE, but she could not tell where this road led off to. It was much too secluded for her to see anything past the mouth of its roadway. It seemed close to another mile before she saw yet another road leading off the main path, with a sign on it that read DEACON McKENZIE.

Driving past this road, she could faintly make out a house in the background, a huge white farmhouse. With several more bends in the road, she at last came to another hard-panned dirt road. The sign on the mouth of this road said JOSH McKENZIE.

Turning the car onto this road, she found that yet again this was also a long dirt pathway. At last, she could see the house as she drove the car around yet another bend in the road. The girls started to squeal in the back seat, excited by the fact they were finally there. Before her was a large pond sitting just feet in front of the house.

"Man, I can't wait to tell everyone about this at school," Jessica screamed out as she departed the car before Deedra had even taken the Silver Lexus out of drive.

"This is way cool! Look at this house! Wow, Casey, look, look at the horses!"

"Wait up, Jessie!" Casey yelled to her sister.

Any thoughts Deedra had, abruptly ended as they came closer to the ranch house. There must have been twenty or more horses grazing in the sectioned-off pastures that surrounded the outer perimeter of the house. As she blinked with wonder, the feeling of peace and tranquility fell suddenly upon her. She brought her attention back to the house and was lost for words. She was absolutely astonished at the size of the house. It was massive for a country home, a large two-story ranch house with a wraparound porch all painted in blue with white accents. The porch had a beautiful rustic appearance, as though the paint were put on years and years before and then allowed to weather. She believed it was purposely made to look this way to add to the overall feel of the home. She loved how the large old oak and pine trees surrounded the home's exterior, while bringing with them the feeling of serenity. Although, even with all of the trees, there was not one that blocked the home's rare beauty. Words could never do this place justice, she thought.

She was still unsure about all of this, and why on earth she was here. If she had only told the children no, all of this could have been avoided. The worst of it, though, was that the children had already met up with Josh's boys, Darrin and Dusty, and were running down to see the horses. Deedra stood there by herself, the nervous apprehension closing in on her.

"Why didn't you tell me about all of this?" Deedra asked as Josh came toward her from the house.

"Would it have made much of a difference if I had?"

Deedra shrugged her shoulders, not really having an answer, but trying desperately just to hold on to her composure and not let him know how odd she felt by being here. What she really wanted was to turn tail and run, go home, back to where she was the safest. She wanted to hide behind the closed doors of her own home. Nevertheless, she was here, and she needed to make the most of it and not let him see just how anxious she really was feeling.

"Well, let's go inside and I'll show you around!" he exclaimed with an urgency to show her his home.

If Deedra thought the outside was impressive, the inside was to die for. The dining room was to be the first part of their tour. As they walked into the room, she looked around and admired the room's hard oak walls and ceiling. The ceiling was in a cathedral design that made the room appear to be even larger than it already was.

Moving from room to room, she noticed that the floors throughout the home, such as the dining room, were done in a beautiful hardwood. She guessed them to be made of oak as well. There were occasional oriental throw rugs here and there. All the walls appeared to be done in tongue and groove, which perfectly matched the coloring of the hardwood floors.

Josh played the perfect host, showing her around the house. It was beautiful. There was a huge stone fireplace in the living room, an oak one in the family room and another oak-mantled one in the master bedroom.

Upon entering the front door, Deedra was so overwhelmed by the inside décor, she had failed to notice the staircase that they were now beginning their journey on. The staircase was made of a dark mahogany and seem to have been handcrafted.

The master bedroom, Josh's room, was extremely large with a king-sized, four-poster bed dominating its space. It was so manly looking, and yet decorated smartly, as though a woman might have designed it.

Deedra took in a deep breath. *Oh God, the room smells of him, it's the same intoxicating aroma.* Knowing this was his domain was making her feel a bit uncomfortable. In fact, being alone with Josh in any room made her feel uneasy. "This is all very beautiful, Josh. You have wonderful taste."

The anger that she had felt toward him on the drive out was now all but gone; she was actually feeling more comfortable around him. She still did not like the idea that he had used the children against her, but she decided that at the appropriate time she would tell him never to do something like that again. She darn sure didn't like the thought of being alone with him, though. She wished the children would come back up closer to where she was. So far, he had not done anything out of the ordinary to make her feel afraid of him.

The more time he spent with her, the better he liked it. He took her down to the horse barn, then to the calf barn. She laughed at his jokes; she talked to the calves in a little girl's voice that was so endearing. He chuckled to himself at how cute she really was. It made him want her even more. Every inch of him wanted so badly to touch her, grab her up in his arms and kiss her. It was all he could do not to.

"Hey, let's go for a ride," Josh said, interrupting her concentration with the calves.

"What? Oh no! I mean—what about the kids?" she stammered, quickly trying to come up with reasons why they should not go.

"The kids will be fine, my boys know this ranch like the back of their hands," he answered.

"I really don't want to leave my girls alone, what if something were to happen?" she asked, her voice nervous.

"Oh come on, the kids will be fine, we won't be gone long! I'll call my brother, Deacon, he will keep an eye out for them. Come on, I want to show you the ranch."

Before she had time to even comprehend what he was doing, Josh was saddling up the horses for the ride. The larger horse was a black and white paint, with beautifully designed features across his sides and neck. Josh told her his name was Tanker. He was Josh's favorite, a gelding, the only one he had ridden for years. The other horse that he was saddling up for her was named Maggie. She was a sweet young mare, three years old, and a paint as well. There were large red splashes of color mixed against her white hair.

Deedra finally felt as though she were starting to relax again, fully enjoying the ride. It had been many years since she had been on the back of a horse, and she amazed herself that she remembered what to do. She was also feeling a bit more relaxed around Josh as he explained pieces of land they covered and what it meant to him.

His stories were full of wonderful memories that he had been fortunate to be apart of, stories that most people would never see, let alone live. The ranch land was large and beautiful with its landscape of trees, fencing and ponds of every size sprinkled throughout its lush green surroundings. Beautiful large oaks and pines were scattered all around with palmetto patches mixed in.

Riding past his father's homestead, Josh relayed yet another story of his father and mother's meeting. Deedra imagined her as a young bride coming to live in her new home and how magnificent of a home it must have been to her back in those days. How proud the elder McKenzie must have been in building his home for his young bride.

She watched with intent as Josh spoke of his parents, especially of his mother, and she could see in his eyes how much he truly admired and loved her. He was so different in many ways from what she would have ever thought him to be.

He was still arrogant and domineering as far as she was concerned, too over-powering, and so excessively sure of himself. Yet he had a softer, almost boylike quality to him that she doubted many people ever saw. There was a charming boy with big bright flashing eyes that emerged when he spoke of his childhood and his family. It was truly an endearing quality.

Maybe he wasn't as bad as she originally thought he was, she rationalized to herself while still taking in the peaceful landscape.

Suddenly the pangs of guilt took hold of her once again and pushed the pleasant moment she was having aside. *A relationship with such a man is unthinkable, I should have known better than this. I made a promise to Craig; I plan to keep it until I die!*

"What you thinking about over there, girl?" Josh's voice broke through her train of thought.

"Oh, oh nothing, just enjoying the ride, it's so beautiful here," she fibbed, feeling a little startled by his voice.

Josh nodded in agreement, then went right in to yet another sweet story about his past. Relaxing her mind once again, listening intently to his stories while she looked out over the vast land before them, she did not notice that Josh had stopped. Deedra turned her horse back around to find that Josh had dismounted and was standing next to his horse.

"Let's give 'em a break, Sunshine."

Deedra's heart immediately skipped a beat; her pulse rose, thinking about the position she was in out there in the middle of all this land. The apprehensiveness took over within her all over again.

Stop here? She thought for a moment. "Out here?" she spoke out, just above a whisper.

"Yes, here! Come on down, Deedra," he said, motioning with his hand toward the ground below. His voice dropped to an urgent hiss, sounding lower and huskier than she had heard it before, only adding to her apprehensive feeling. The tone of his voice sent a shudder up her spine.

By no means did she want to get down off the horse. Her heart was racing rapidly at the notion of them being alone here; she was terrified of what might happen. No one was close enough to offer her any protection.

Josh reached for her hand, sending a shock wave of want deep into her belly immediately. God, she hated the feeling of having no control. His big hand engulfed hers, the skin rough and callused, so absolutely male. Every indicator light that could go off in Deedra's brain was bleeping harder than ever before, the caution flags rising up all around her, the walls closing in trying to guard and protect. Yet, even with all of the warnings her mind was signaling, she dismounted the horse, only to plant her feet on the ground just inches away from him.

Without a word, he pulled her into him, his large arms holding her body tightly against him, taking her breath away. She felt her pulse double; she inhaled sharply. Deedra took a step to move away, without really fighting. But he brought her closer in to him, keeping their bodies aligned and her securely in his embrace.

She tried to break free, tried to push away from him without actually struggling. She knew he was much too close for comfort, and yet not close enough. Her body wanted to feel him against her, but in spite of that, her mind was telling her this could not be allowed. His grasp was hot and electrifying, and an involuntary tingle surged through her body; it terrified her.

The beat of her heart was felt in her throat, and she was struggling desperately to take her breaths in and out. She had the feeling as though she might fall from her legs starting to shake. She pushed against him, trying to break free of the hold he had over her, and then realized the struggling she thought she was doing to break free was only in her mind. In actuality, she was not trying to get loose at all.

The scent of his body filled the air around her again, this time so real, so close, it was intoxicating her mind. The little hairs on the back of her neck were standing at attention.

Josh turned her face up from his chest to look directly at him. She focused what consciousness she had left on where the black pupil ended and the deep dark brown of his eye color began. Framing her face in his hands, he found her mouth with his thumbs, tracing the moist softness of her lips with his fingers.

"I have to kiss you!"

"Josh, no!" she heard herself say.

He brought his lips to hers anyway. Barely touching her, he took the words in her mouth away with the slightest brush of warmth. His kiss tasted dangerous and forbidden. He brought his right hand to the back of her head, allowing the left one to move slowly to the small of her back, bringing her body even closer to his. Holding her weight against him, her feet barely touched the ground.

The look in his eyes was mesmerizing; she could not keep from staring into them. His lips brushed against her lips again. Tenderly, sweetly. He knew how to kiss. Soft, nibbling bites to her full pouty lips that turned into slow, erotic glides with his tongue against the sensitive wetness, then becoming a deep tangled mesh of tongues. His mouth was like fire on hers, his breath burning.

For a short instant, she regained her senses and she tried to break free, bringing her arms up to push him back away from her. He held her tighter still, putting his fingers deep within her golden curls, causing her to gasp for air.

When he bent his face in to kiss her this time, he kissed the soft full lips harder, demanding her mouth to open to him. She tried to move her face away, not allow another kiss to happen. But she couldn't. Her mouth belonged in his power, the red-hot feeling of his lips on hers.

"Josh—" she muttered.

He stared at her as if dazed for a moment, his chest heaving beneath his tight shirt.

"Shhh, Don't say it, Deedra! Please, baby, don't…"

He took his hand from behind her head, reached up to his own head, removed the cowboy hat and threw it out into the grassy field. Deedra watched with intent as the long black hair fell down around his shoulders, the glistening from the sun giving the appearance of being a dark blue color.

The fear and the fright seemed to take control of her in ways she never would have expected. Almost like an aphrodisiac urging her to want more. A part of her knew she could stop this, could stop him. She had the power to push him away if she wanted. But she didn't seem to have any command over her own awareness.

Deedra found herself melting into his strong arms as the kisses became more urgent, intense and demanding. Her mouth searched his lips as urgently as his searched hers. Her breathing became sharp and labored. She held tightly to him, thinking that she might faint; her heart pounded hard in her chest.

It had been a long time since she had been with a man, and never in her existence had a kiss felt like this. The need, the desire, clouded her senses, overpowering her intelligence of what she thought was right or wrong. There was not one thing she could do to stop the jolt of pleasure that surged through her veins. Nor could she stop the deep-rooted longing that tied her passion into a tangled web of confusion and burning need.

Before she had a chance to comprehend all that was happening to her, Josh removed his shirt, exposing his rock hard muscles. Without a word, he undid the button on his jeans and quickly removed them. He wan't wearing any underwear. He was standing there naked before her.

She struggled for breath at the sight of his lower torso. Quickly, Josh dropped to his knees, taking her with him, and then laid her down in the tall blanket of grass. Feverishly he kissed her lips, neck and shoulder blades—anything not covered by clothing. He was careful not to miss any of the supple flesh left exposed by her shirt.

He turned his attentions to the soft fabric of the shirt lying softly against her breast. Lightly he bit at the swollen nipple with just enough pressure to make her want even more. Moving from the nipple to the soft areas of her body, he lightly bit at the surrounding areas of the breast, then her arms and back up to her mouth for a short bite to the bottom lip. Then he repeated the process again.

Her body had never throbbed like this, the sound and the thump of the beat of her heart. There was an unmistakable ache, as if she would turn to flames if the cravings were not quenched. She closed her eyes, focusing only on the new feelings she was experiencing.

It was frightening that he was capable of controlling her body like this. Deedra was sure he was destroying her with these deliciously decadent sensations. The fierce desires deviously filled her thoughts.

At first, the touches to her skin were tender, almost as if she were a small flower in his hands. But, in actuality it was all he could do to be gentle. What he really wanted was to devour every inch of her as quickly as he could. Patience, he was desperately trying to be patient. He knew he must make her wait; he wanted her to desire him with a passion unlike anything ever felt before. He wanted her to remember this moment in her mind for a lifetime. He had the urge to make her beg, to cry out his name in the midst of her lust. She had to succumb to the pleasures. Deedra had to be his.

Masterfully, Josh unbuttoned the silken blouse. Deedra let out a small moan as he removed it quickly from her arms and tossed it aside. Sitting her up a bit, he reached behind her and unsnapped the pale pink bra, haphazardly throwing it in the direction of the shirt. Tenderly he kissed and manipulated the areas left exposed, another nip here or there with his teeth to the soft flesh, then he let his lips and tongue kiss the areas. Slowly he suckled each nipple to their full pulsating hardness and then he would stop and nip at them once again. Lying on the thick grass, Deedra let out a moan of desire.

Josh positioned himself to the foot of her; then bent over her waist to remove her jeans. Swiftly removing them and sliding them down and off of her, he left only the matching pale pink panties behind.

Deliberately, he let his hair touch everything his hands and mouth tasted. She was so beautiful to him, the look of innocence, wide-eyed and yet so very sensual.

Deedra didn't know what she was supposed to feel at this moment. She only knew it was a relentless mixture of fright coupled with an overpowering ache running through her veins for him to continue.

The peach-colored skin of her body glowed where the sun shone on it. Stunningly, she lay there before him. Everywhere he touched her felt like fire under his fingertips. Kneeling over top of her, his legs resting on either side of her waist, he caressed each breast, marveling at their shape. They were perfectly round and generously proportioned, a strikingly delicate soft peach in color with small, deep mauve-colored areolas and large expressive nipples.

He let his tongue swirl around the outside of the areola, letting it quickly flick the nipple now and then. He could tell by the movements of her body that she was craving for more than he was giving to her just yet. He had a plan. One that included taking his sweet time with this exquisite woman, savoring every inch of her delicious essence.

He let his tongue lick around the breast again slowly, careful to cover everything but the nipple itself this time. Deedra grabbed for his head, pushing it to her breast with force. She needed to feel the intensity of his touch. He resisted her, not allowing her the control. He wanted her to experience the torment of the wait, allowing only for the slow whispered moans coming from Deedra's throat to tell him how much stimulation each area of her body needed. He teased and tortured. Made her hunger for him. He enjoyed hearing her beg for him in the low throaty moan.

Moving himself down between her thighs, he gently slipped the panties gradually down her legs, kissing each of her inner thighs as he did so. At first, she resisted a little. Her muscles rigid against his touch, he gently opened her legs to him. Perhaps the muscles were so inflexible because of the small amount of concern showing in her eyes. Possibly no one had ever touched her like this with their hands in this way, or if they did, it had been so many years before.... He didn't know.

He had the feeling it was the latter. No one had touched her this intimately in a long time, not even her own hands had delved into this area. Gently he probed the silkiness of her with his large middle finger, Moving it slowly in and out of the sweltering flesh, feeling the slick, wet, pulsating heat as it intensified. Josh could feel her back start to arch. He backed off instantly, wanting her to be held back from the orgasm she so desperately desired.

He wanted her to feel as alive and free as she possibly could. The release could not come just yet; he wanted to see the inhibitions release themselves from her soul first.

Bringing her hips up a little, holding her up with his strong hands, he brought his face down between her thighs. Slowly, methodically, he tongued the sweet wetness lightly, flickering, letting his tongue lap at the small hood with just enough pressure for her to know he was there, making each sensation she felt more intense. Soft moaning sounds escaped her lips. Josh smiled to himself; this was what he wanted from her. To forget who she was and just go with the passion, be a impious woman.

Reveling in the amplified moisture, he drove his tongue in and out with increased pressure, lightly licking upward on the inner walls, then circling the hood, then going back down. He repeated it over and over.

When he was sure she was close to exploding, he started back up her body, searching out her mouth, demanding her to kiss him. Then again, he slowly flicked his tongue, tickling her lightly all the way down to where he had just been. Her hips started moving in unison with his tongue, her gasp for air was heavier, her moans low and throaty. He knew the inhibitions had been released, the only thing left was the demand to be pleased.

It would not be long before she would finally beg for what he knew she really wanted, needed. Pressing his tongue hard against the sweet spot, he let it encircle the flowering hood. He would wait until her hips started to thrust upwards before he would stop. Josh let out a low, evil-sounding laugh, listening to the intense sounds from her throat.

Putting his large hands on her breast, he lightly pinched them as he devoured her with harder pressure from his tongue against her flesh. Deedra's legs were almost up to her chest, her body rocking with the overwhelming feelings he was sending through her like an electrical charge. He patiently waited, listening for her despite the fact that the pulsating manhood between his legs was trying to make him lose control of his mind and just take her.

"Please, please. God, please," she hoarsely repeated.

"You want me? You're sure?" he teased, already knowing the answer.

"Yes, Josh." The words were subdued, but he heard them loud and clear.

Josh brought her legs down from where they had been bent up toward her chest and turned her over on her stomach with one fast flip. He then raised her hips. She didn't know what he planned to do in this stance, but she didn't try to move from the strange new position. She didn't say anything, not a word. All he heard was her moaning for him.

He wanted to shove himself in her, but he had enough forethought left about him to realize that he was a largely built man, and it was possible she may have not had a man of his size.

He started slowly, easing his way in to make room for himself, allowing the head to be inserted and brought out several times, then putting a little more in and then pulling almost all the way back out. Finally, he was sure she was wet and more than ready.

He thrust back in, all the way this time with force. She exploded; the cry echoed through the woods, and then was quickly replaced with a low, cat-like growl.

Continuing the movement repeatedly, he pulled almost all the way out and then thrust himself back in again. He watched her body as it pushed against him, wanting more. Four more climaxes took hold of her before he allowed the release of his own lifeblood deep within her, leaving her body silent and drained.

Chapter 10

Deedra frantically tried to compose herself, removing the leaves and grass from her body and hair. She did not want the children to see her like this, did not want them to ask any questions, did not want anyone to ask. Smugly Josh lay there watching her dress; she was everything he had imagined her to be. She would be his now, his for a lifetime. Deedra's only thoughts were of how self-satisfied he looked, so content with himself and what he had done.

Damn him! she thought to herself, biting on her lower lip. Damn herself, how could she have let this happen? Her own mind and body had failed her.

He made her feel things she had never before experienced in her life, passion and desire like she only dreamed of lately with him, and imagined only happened in the romance novels she read.

He had taken control of her, and she had let him.

As quickly as the sensations had thrust her into a new and exciting world, she was cast back down again just as rapidly. Suddenly the guilt was back, looming over her head like vultures waiting to attack their prey. It was dark and evil. She was no better than a whore now, she reasoned. A disgrace to her husband's memory, and of what was morally right or wrong.

She never wanted any of this. She was so confused by these thoughts; they threatened all that had been safe to her. She was at a loss for the moment as to why she did what she had with Josh.

Back on their horses, riding without a spoken word between them, they stopped close to where the children were playing near one of the ponds. They were laughing and having a wonderful time trying to fish. They were very unaware of the solemn mood Deedra was in; her mind was a million miles away. Try as she might to watch the children play, her thoughts would not leave her alone. Every fragment of her existence could sense the areas Josh had touched. Her body had been awakened for the first time in its life, and it was begging to have more. The ache was deep within.

Intellectually she knew there could be no future. But mentally, her mind was playing wicked tricks. It craved for Josh to control her again—to feel possessed and dominated. The thoughts of the wonderful sensations haunted her.

She told herself that now was not the time to set things right with Josh. He would have to understand that what happened earlier was a huge mistake. It would be wrong to allow him to think that a relationship between them could go any further. It could never happen again. She had to make sure that it was clear and defined, that indeed this had been wrong, that there was absolutely no future for them.

Deedra headed back up to the house under the pretense of using the bathroom. She needed time to think. She had to find the right words to say to Josh to make him understand. She did not want to hurt him, but he had to know as quickly as possible that they could not see each other again. No sooner did the front screen door shut, than she heard it open again and turned to see Josh coming through it behind her. Without pretense he walked over to where she was standing. He reached out to take her in his arms and kiss her, but she moved her head away. She pushed herself away from his touch.

"No, Josh, the kids!" Then she realized she had to say more than just that. She had to try to be honest.

"You're assuming way too much from me," she tried explaining, pushing away from his grasp again.

My God! Where's the woman I was just with? Where did she go? We were just together an hour or so ago, and she is already adding disclaimers? Josh thought, a look of disbelief on his face.

"Look, I thought—"

"I know what you must have thought!" Deedra cut him off in mid-sentence. "This just isn't right, I mean—I'm sorry about today. We should have never—"

"Never what?" he asked, his voice raised. "Never what, Deedra?"

"This isn't right, that's all! It should never have happened," she rationalized.

Josh grabbed for her, kissing her hard on the mouth, then releasing her just as quickly. "Now, what's not right about it?"

"Damn you, don't you—" A look of instant anger crossed her face. "Don't you dare do that again!"

"Don't I dare? I'll be darned if I understand you, your sayin' this ain't right, I haven't even started yet, lady!" he snapped back.

"Jo—"

Josh cut off the words before she could even begin to explain. "Look, I needed you, you needed me! I saw it in your eyes. I don't play games, little girl! If I want something, I go after it! But, I've been pussy-footin' around with your ass for months trying to get you to notice! And now, what? You're saying it ain't right? What the hell is that about?" He was being vindictive, the words flowing from his tongue in rapid speed.

"Look, you don't understand," Deedra snapped. "I shouldn't have even come out here. I knew better! I don't want a relationship with you! You or anyone!"

"Well, you know what, Deedra, I don't get it! Out there," Josh pointed toward the back door, "you gave yourself to me, you came out of your damn shell you've got yourself boxed into! You wanted it, wanted me—I know it! Now you're standin' here actin' like I've got the plague or something, saying there isn't even a chance?"

"It just happened." She tried to reason with him, repeating her words. "I'm not looking for a relationship. Look, I shouldn't have come—"

Josh cut her off again, even angrier than before. His ego was bruised. His face flushed deep red. "Well, when the hell are you gonna be ready? How many years you want me to give you? Damn, I been playin' this game of chase for months! Like I had nothing better to do than come to your damn restaurant!" He was pacing the floor by now, the rage strong and forthcoming. "Gawd, I'm stupid, I can't believe I've fallen for a woman that's still pinin' away for a dead man! *A dead man!*" He said it more for himself than actually for her, but he immediately realized he shouldn't have said it. With the immediate burst of tears, he knew he had cut Deedra to the bone. He hadn't meant to hurt her like that, it was just the fury talking.

"Look, just forget about the pizza tonight, I will explain to the kids! I'm going home!" Deedra was drying the tears, and she headed for the door in one swift movement. He didn't try to stop her. The rage he was feeling at the moment overshadowed everything. He was not about to beg her to stay and talk about it any further.

Chapter 11

With the children bathed and in bed, Deedra drew the hottest bath her body could stand, hoping that the water would ease the tenseness she was feeling.

Easing herself into the water, she grit her teeth and felt the deep burn against her skin. Tears of frustration started streaming down her cheeks immediately. Her thoughts focused back on what happened earlier with Josh. Was he right about what he said? Or just trying to hurt her? Why didn't he leave her alone in the first place? None of this would be happening. *God, what Craig must be thinking of me? I acted like some wanton whore; and I knew better.* The tears fell harder the more she thought about what she had done.

A part of her was ashamed of the emotions she had displayed. Although, at the same time, she had needed what had happened. The conflict she fought with only made the pain that more difficult to comprehend. She was fighting back and forth with emotions she couldn't quite understand. Finally she came to the decision that she must never allow herself to see Josh in any capacity ever again. If he came into the Fireside, then she would go to the back of the restaurant and wait for him to leave. She would avoid him from now on.

Deedra toweled herself off, much too exhausted to dress. The house was dark except from the shadows playing against the walls from the moon. Pulling the dark blue pillow soft comforter down on the bed, she slid between the cotton sheets. The towel was still wrapped around her body. Totally drained of emotion, sleep claimed her.

The knock on the front door startled her awake. Everything was dark around her. On impulse she looked over at the small clock on the nightstand; it was three-thirty in the morning.

She lay there, cautiously listening, thinking maybe she really didn't hear the sound. The knocking sound happened again, and for a brief second she was paralyzed, wondering who would be at the door at this hour. A prowler? Someone with the intentions to rob her?

Deedra slowly rose from the bed, making her steps light and airy so as not to be heard. Quietly she let the towel she had secured around her drop to the floor, and then she reached for her robe. Hurriedly she threw it on, tying the long strap around her tightly. In the still of the night, with only the moon's reflection to guide her, she eased into the living room, hoping to reach the door before the next knock woke the children up.

"Who's there?" she whispered, her face against the door, trying to see in the little peephole as to who was outside. "Who's there, I said?"

The low husky voice answered her. "It's Josh, let me in! I need to speak to you."

"No, Josh, go home! It's too late for you to be here!" Her voice became a little more elevated.

"I'm not going anywhere till you open the door! Come on, Deedra, open the door!"

"No!" she said, her voiced raised. "I said go home! Just go home, Josh."

"If you don't let me in I'm gonna start hollering out here!" he declared louder.

Now what do I do? I do not want the neighbors to be woken. How embarrassing that would be if they saw him outside at this time of night. I would be the center of gossip for the next year. Reluctantly she opened the door just a bit. "What do you want?" she asked through the half-opened door, staring at him coldly.

"I had to see you and apologize for what I said," Josh replied, trying to whisper. He had done nothing else but think about what had happened earlier that day. When he could not rest, he decided to go for

71

a drive, and he had ended up at Deedra's front step. He had to apologize for the hateful words he spoke.

"Then you should have called," Deedra snapped sharply.

"Well I couldn't, I didn't have your number!" he said, realizing she had only cracked the door by inches and was not about to let him in her house.

"Just go home, will you please? I'm tired, I don't want to deal with this right now."

Deedra never got to finish what she was trying to say. Pushing with his weight against the door, it opened a little wider. Reaching with his arm extended he found her head, bringing his hand behind it. Then he brought her face close to his. Though she fought a little to release her head from his grasp, his mouth connected with hers forcefully. Deedra stopped resisting for the moment, allowing the passionate heat of the kiss to envelop her. Her intake of breath was labored. Coming to her senses, she suddenly pulled her head to the side and away from his grasp.

"Damn you! Leave me the hell alone! Why can't you understand? Just leave me alone!" Deedra grit her teeth forcefully together, totally beside herself with ferocity. She despised him, hated everything about him, and yet, she gave in to the touch of his lips.

For Josh, it just was not that easy to let go of her; he was sure he was already in love. He didn't want to walk out and never see her again. He was desperately afraid that if he stepped his foot back from the door and she closed it, it would close any impending future he thought they may have.

"Deedra, please listen—"

"Not another word, Josh, just go!" She glared at him irately.

Damn it! I have to get through to her somehow. If she won't let me talk then I will show her, he contemplated.

Just as the thought crossed his mind, he realized the door was still slightly ajar, and he pushed with all his weight through its threshold. Deedra was flabbergasted, completely stunned by the audacity he had.

This time when he reached out for her face, he did so with urgency, taking her face in both of his hands, then bringing her close to him. For a split second, he looked into her eyes, catching Deedra in his hypnotic spell. The look in his eyes seemed wicked. Her mind fought to resist again, but didn't; she was mesmerized instead by his gaze. Her body relaxed into him, again falling victim to his fiery kisses.

Once again, her willful mind commanded her to stop him, fight the yield of his power over her. She wrestled away from his grasp.

"Get out of here, now!" Deedra shouted, angrier than before. "Go!" She pushed at his large frame to back it out of the door's entryway, making him even more infuriated. "I said go!"

With no forethought, just as he had done early in the day, he unleashed the angry words from his mouth.

"Forget you, Deedra, damn! One minute you look at me like you want me bad, the next you're pushing me away like I'm trash! You have got to be the most dim-witted woman I have ever known in my life! I don't need you or your stupid problems, I can get ten women in your place tomorrow and not have them carry so much baggage. So you know what, Deedra, screw your problems and your crap!"

Deedra didn't utter a word. She stood there, frightened, looking down at the floor. Never had she known someone this angry. No one had ever said so much as a cross word to her, let alone raised his or her voice like this.

"Go on living the way you are, in some damn dark hole!" Josh continued, some of the rage subsiding. "You think you're some princess or something. My Gawd, everyone calls you 'Ice Princess' anyway, and now I know why!"

"What?" she asked, stunned by the fact that anyone would call her such a thing. "What did you say?"

"Ice Princess Deedra, you heard me the first time! The Ice Princess!" he repeated again, dragging the words out slowly as if she lacked intelligence.

"No one calls me that! That's a lie you're making up to hurt me!"

"A lie? No, Deedra, sorry, it's the truth! You think you are some kind of princess, you act like you're some kind of princess—that's for sure! Gawd knows you don't need the likes of someone like me, right Ms. Debutante?" He grabbed for her again, catching her face roughly in his large hands. He pressed his face to hers. She turned away from him so that he could not kiss her. Pursing his mouth hard against her cheek, he spoke in a low, whispered snarl.

"I am so tired of watching you from afar, like some kind of sick stalker, while you just go on with life like I'm not even here! I didn't go to the restaurant just so I could see you for a minute at a time, I went there…I went there because I wanted you, thought I was falling in love…" His teeth clenched as the words tried to spill out through his wrath.

He paused for a few moments, collecting his thoughts, trying his best to calm himself. He hoped beyond hope that something he had said would trigger her to feel something. Maybe even change her mind about him, make her say she wanted him as well. Yet she said nothing. She just stood there, blank and angry. There was no motion, no words—nothing to give him hope. The last few months of waiting, of hoping she would have feeling for him, was now all on the line. This was the final moment as far as he was concerned. If the daily visits to see her for whatever time she allowed, if the passion shared out in the pasture did not sway her, then nothing ever would. She would never identify with the blinding feelings a man could experience for a woman. She would never realize how his heart ached at times to be near her, if only for a few seconds. He had wished that one day, in the midst of the last few months, she would feel just a little of what he felt for her.

Josh dropped his hands from her face. He waited silently for her to say something. Yet, her silence filled the space around them.

"I'm a stupid idiot, aren't I? I never had a chance with a cold hearted bitch like you!"

The door slammed hard against its frame, startling Deedra. Her knees went weak instantaneously; she let her body slide down the wall in to a squatting position on the floor. Hysterically the sobs began, hard and fierce. The sorrow in her heart was intense. Her body started to quiver; the thoughts in her mind rattled.

There was nothing she could have said to Josh. Nothing she could have told him. There were no words for what was going on inside of her. All she could comprehend was that he was able to touch her in ways she had never before experienced in her life, and it was threatening what was supposed to be her simple existence.

She hated him and should be thankful that he would finally leave her alone and let her go back to the way things were. He was too passionate and unyielding, much too temperamental and arrogant. He was rowdy and loud. He angered too quickly. He cut too hard with his words.

She hated him because of what he did to her. He terrified her because of his ability to make her do things she did not want to do. He made her crave him. Every chance he had that his lips touched hers, she forgot who she was. He was an evil man, with his power to take control and dominate her. It was the only clear answer to what she allowed him to do out in that pasture. She hated him for making her into something she was never meant to be. Yet, in spite of all that, her heart felt as though it were being torn to shreds.

Deedra composed herself, stood up, and quietly walked back to the bedroom. The sobs became slow burning tears. Carefully, as though she would fall apart if she moved too quickly, she eased herself back into the bed, the safe haven, the hiding zone of her life. Like a small child afraid of the thunder, she curled herself up into a ball, holding her pillow for dear life. She willed herself to quiet the tears and relax her body.

Who was he? What was he? Why did he have to come into her life? she questioned herself. The tears started again, stinging her eyes. The anger welled up again. "YOU DON'T UNDERSTAND! NO ONE UNDERSTANDS!" she screamed out and then realized what she had done; there was no one to hear her. *It's better this way. Love me, huh? You would only hurt me in the end*, she thought. Her mind felt total confusion; possibly, she was losing her mind, going crazy. The pain welled up from somewhere deep inside. She was unsure of who or what she was actually crying over; Josh, Craig or herself.

Chapter 12

Morning came too swiftly for Deedra. She hurried the children off to school as quickly as she could, then called into work, saying she was ill and would not be in. Going into the bathroom she looked at her refection in the mirror; her eyes were swollen from the tears shed the night before.

She was so pale, tired, and mentally drained. She had the feeling of being on the verge of a breakdown. Something was wrong, though she didn't have a clue what it was exactly. Why had she cried so hard through the night? There were so many odd emotions, but none she was able to comprehend.

Calling Marcy at home, she explained that she wasn't feeling well and would not be in to work. She asked her if she could take over her shift for the day. Her friend could hear something wrong in Deedra's voice and told her she would be by to see her before going to work. Deedra was glad of that. She desperately needed her friend today. At the close of the conversation, she climbed back into her safe place.

When no answer came to the door, Marcy started to worry. She let herself in and went in search of Deedra. It was almost noon, and there was no sound coming from anywhere in the house. Marcy found Deedra asleep and woke her.

"You had me worried, are you all right?" Marcy looked at her, staring at the swollen eyes and dark circles on Deedra's face. "What is wrong with you?"

Silently the tears welled up in Deedra's eyes.

"Deedra, you're scaring me, what's wrong with you?"

With that, the silent tears turned to intense sobs. Through the sobs, she tried to explain everything that had happened the day before and then again early this morning. Her words were jumbled; Marcy strained to understand what she was trying to say.

"Oh my God, did he rape you?" Marcy demanded, not totally understanding everything with clarity, her own voice breaking up. "Well, did he, Deedra?"

"No, no! Marcy, no! I allowed this, I allowed him to."

Marcy took a deep breath, exhaling slowly, the initial fear of what happened to her friend answered. After calming Deedra down, she was able to figure out everything she had been trying to tell her. Marcy went to the kitchen and fixed Deedra a strong cup of tea. When it was ready, she brought it back to her.

"Drink this; you'll feel better, it will calm you. Want me to fix you something to eat?"

"No, I'm just glad you're here!"

"You know, Deedra..." Marcy started to speak cautiously, realizing that the wrong words would set her off, and yet Deedra needed to hear what was on her mind. "I'm not trying to upset you." Marcy positioned herself next to Deedra on the edge of the bed. "Some of what Josh is saying is true."

She stopped to see if Deedra would have a reaction to her words, cut in to her and get angry for meddling. When she realized Deedra wasn't going to argue yet, she continued to tell her friend the thoughts she had.

"I mean, I'm not saying he's right or wrong, or that his methods are right. But, you have held on to the past for a long time, Deedra."

Deedra just lay there motionless, listening to her.

"No matter what, I don't think Craig would have liked this—your hanging on like this, I mean. For years, not living..."

A spark of irritation started to shine in Deedra's eyes.

"Look, before you get angry, just let me finish. It's not Craig's death that shut you down, it's the fact that he was safe. The fact that you didn't have to do anything with Craig but live in this bubble.

Being sheltered from life, you know what I mean? But now, you're like—well, living this slow death. Waiting, waiting on—" Marcy stopped for a moment, looking at Deedra, watching the reactions to her face. She knew she had upset her with her words, but it was the truth, even if Deedra didn't see it. "Waiting on death! There, I said it."

"What on earth are you talking about? I live every day, work every day! I'm happy, at least I was till he came around! Until he came into my life! Deedra quipped back, so sure she had all of the answers. Unfortunately, Marcy wasn't buying any of her reasonings.

"Deedra, are you kidding me? You don't even try to live—haven't lived in years." Marcy's voice was a bit elevated. "Look, I'm not saying Josh is right for you. Then again, maybe I am saying it too. I mean, he is the first man you've looked at without looking past them like they didn't exist. All he's done wrong, really, is threatened your feeling of safety! And no, Deedra, you're not living—you're existing! There's a huge difference!"

"No, this is his fault, it's all his fault," Deedra interrupted. "He even had the audacity to call me an ice princess, even said others were calling me that. But I know he was just trying to hurt me—"

"Wait a minute, Deedra, how are your insecurities his fault?" Marcy interrupted, focusing on that sentence. "He didn't make you shut down; you did that all by yourself! And yes, Deedra, everyone does call you the Ice Princess, Josh was telling the truth about that."

"Oh Marcy, no! Who would say such a thing?"

"It's a joke everyone shares, Deedra, long before Josh ever came into the picture. You're cold as ice to any man, every man that comes near you."

Deedra stared at her friend in disbelief.

"Look, you can't blame Josh for your actions, or I should say lack there of. It's not his responsibility that you can't let go of the past—a past you were never happy with in the first place."

"What?" Deedra's voice became elevated. "How can you say I wasn't happy? I loved Craig. I was very happy!"

"I disagree, Deedra. I'm sorry, but I do! You were lonely and afraid, he took advantage of it like an old perv and you let him! You were treated like a child by him and you liked the feeling of safety, so you never questioned it."

"Marcy that's a damn lie! Where do you come up with such crap? I married him because I loved him, period! You just never liked Craig, never gave him a chance!"

"Oh, OK, Deedra, if you say so. I'm not about to argue with you about this, or Craig for that matter. We have always disagreed about Craig, always will. Besides, you seem to always know better than anyone." Marcy stood from the bed and started for the bedroom door. "Look, I'm going to go, I will check on you later."

Marcy figured that no matter what she said, Deedra would have a different perspective about it. Before leaving, she arranged to have the children spend the night after school at Mrs. Baker's house. Marcy was hoping this would give Deedra time to her thoughts.

Deedra laid her head back on the pillow, allowing the silence to fill the room. She did not want to think. She wanted only for sleep to claim her. She was much too tired for all of this. She needed rest. She desperately just needed some rest.

Two hours passed before Deedra woke again, and the first thoughts on her mind were what Marcy had said earlier...

Was Marcy right? Had she closed herself off? Was Josh threatening her silence in this world? Was he interrupting the safety she needed? No, no, that wasn't it. Couldn't be it. *He is just so rough, unyielding. He does not understand me. Besides, he means nothing to me. Just something I need to forget. I was happy, very happy. What am I saying? I am happy! He just wants something that I am not willing to give.* Deedra psychoanalyzed, making the same excuses repeatedly in her thoughts.

What's more, he doesn't really want me; he just wants to dominate, to control. He cannot control me, cannot have me. Besides, look at all I have done. I take care of my house, my children, my business... How can Marcy say I just exist? I married Craig for life, that's all. I am still his wife; I will always be his wife.

She thought of one excuse after another as to why she was right and why what Marcy and Josh had said was wrong, not realizing the excuses allowed her the ability to not have to surrender herself to what they said, and in many ways, not have to live with it either. It was easier for her to believe that she was meant to live the way she did, easier to convince herself that the world she chose was the right one, and so much easier to discredit the burning words Josh had alleged to her.

Chapter 13

Josh's day was lousy from the moment he stepped outside the house. Already he had been in one argument with Deacon. Afterwards he snapped at his foreman, Pete. If that were not enough to set the day off, he tore his hand open on the bob-wired fence he was repairing. His mood turned sour, so everyone was staying clear of him. His mood was no match for anyone.

"Hey, Josh!" Deacon yelled as he walked toward his brother, deciding to antagonize the situation, as only he loved to do. "Just what is your problem today? You've got everyone keeping their distance."

"Just leave it alone, Deacon, I ain't in no mood," he replied sternly.

"Awe now, little brother, what's a matter?" Deacon was smiling, knowing that talking to him as if he was a little boy only aggravated him more.

"Deacon, I ain't gonna fight with your ass today! Let's just say my mood is horse shit, and I don't want to be bothered, just leave it at that!" Josh snapped.

Deacon grinned one of those Cheshire cat grins and thought to himself, *Hmmmm, this could be fun.*

"Look, Bro, I was just tryin' to help. Must be that pretty lil girl you brought over here, huh? She ruffle your feathers, did she?"

That was it. Deacon hit on the exposed nerve.

"Just get the hell out of here, Deacon, and don't start! I don't want your shit right now! I'll whip your ass standin' right here, right now!"

"Awe now, Josh." Deacon snickered. "You really wanna do that?"

"Yeah, I really wanna do it! I ain't in the mood for this, I mean it." He threw his fence pliers to the ground in anger. "I told you to go on and leave me alone, now do it!" Josh barked, ready to go after his brother if he uttered another word.

Deacon knew from experience going up against his younger brother in several fights that he would do it, there was no doubt in his mind. *Oh hell, he isn't any fun like this,* he reasoned.

Josh could still hear Deacon mumbling something as he walked away. He didn't care what he said as long as he didn't have to hear him right now. He darn sure was in the mood to fight him if he hadn't shut up.

Truth be known, he wished he could talk to somebody, even to Deacon. He wanted to say what was wrong, but he knew Deacon wouldn't care to hear it. After all, he had a good marriage and a good woman. He lived in his nice house and came home every night to the laughter of children and something good to eat on his dinner table.

He had no idea what it was like to be single. He didn't have to go out there and try to find someone to love him, only to find some "half-wit" woman that was after money or a name. Deacon didn't have to search for the woman of his dreams only to find he would be turned down or cast out like yesterday's bad news. Besides, knowing Deacon, he would have just said to leave the woman alone, find someone else. But, it wasn't that easy. This woman had gotten under his skin. However, she had to be the coldest woman he had ever known.

No, that's not true ether, he thought. *She was on fire yesterday. She was passionate. But, she just wasn't going to show it. There is so much fire in this woman to be so damn cold.*

Deedra had bruised his ego, made him feel less of a man than he thought he was. Always, he felt so sure of himself except when he was around her now. One look into her eyes, and he was trapped. He didn't know how the hell it had happened, just that it had.

He hadn't wanted to go there early this morning, hadn't wanted to argue with her. He had wanted her to see how much he wanted her, wanted to be with her.

Instead, what he had found was a venomous snake. Her words had struck him, filling him with poison deep in his veins. He couldn't get her out of his mind, even though he knew he would have to. He had told her early this morning that he would never bother her again, and he meant it. It was time to forget her and go on with life.

Besides, I can get any woman I want. Anytime I want! Why would I need a woman that's so difficult? It's ignorant to work that hard for something when they don't give a damn anyway.

Momma was whistling as he entered the old-fashioned kitchen. Although it had been upgraded many times, the original feel of the house was still evident in the walls and decorations lying about. There was still the same old cook stove sitting off to the side as a decoration now with a brand new one, all white and shiny in its place.

Momma and Daddy had waited a long time after their marriage to bring Deacon and Joshua into the world. They wanted a marriage built on love and trust, not on how many kids they could whelp to do the chores, as they so often did in their day.

Josh always could go to Momma with anything, she always listened, and even though at times she was famous for stepping on his toes, she was right about most everything she said.

"Well hey there, son!" she spoke in her southern twang to him as he sat down at the kitchen table, the smell of a fresh baked apple pie filling the air.

"Hey, Momma, you got time to talk?" Josh asked, sounding like a little boy coming to his mommy with a problem that happened in school.

His mother nodded and went over to the coffee pot and started adding the ingredients. Then she figured she would offer him a piece of peach pie to go with their coffee and conversation.

"Come sit with me, Momma, will you?" he asked, patting the chair next to his.

Katy realized this was not going to be the normal conversation about the ranch. There was urgency to her son's voice.

"OK, what's wrong?" she asked, looking over at him.

Josh began explaining everything to her about Deedra. She had only known bits and pieces of this woman through minor conversations she had with Josh at an early time. Now he was filling her in completely. Everything he felt for her, all the way back to when he first saw her. He told her she was turning his world upside down. How he felt around her. What she smelled like, looked like. He also told her about the last conversation they had, the one before he had slammed the door and walked away.

Katy could see the pain in her son's eyes as he spoke. She even detected a small tear in the corner of his left eye.

It was so much easier when he was little to kiss away the pains. He had been through so much.

Like all mothers, Katy hoped that one day he would find the right woman and be able to settle down and have the family he always wanted to have. She had known from the first minute she laid eyes on his first wife that she was not right for her son, but no amount of telling him would have changed his mind, and he had learned the hard way.

"Josh," his mother broke in. "I'm an old woman, son, looking through these tired eyes at you."

Josh sat there quietly, listening. Momma always had the best advice. However, sometimes you really had to listen closely to get the meanings behind what she said

"This girl you're talkin' about, sounds like she needs love more than you realize. At least, from what you've said to me, anyway, it sounds like you might have something there someday. But, son, you've always been so sure of yourself, and you push for what you want, sometimes push too hard! Sometimes that isn't such a good thing, you can't just push her to get what you want. She's confused, her husband's dead, you know? She's a widow now." Katy stopped talking for a moment, waiting for acknowledgement from Josh as to what she was saying.

"Yes Momma," he answered.

"I kind of know what she feels, I lost your daddy and I thought my world was going to crumble down around me. She's tryin' to be true to her husband, the daddy of her kids. Now here you are traipsing in, tryin' to be in her life, and she is confused, I think. You know what I'm sayin' to you, son?"

"Yeah, I think so."

"Look, son, you can't just grab her up and make her yours just because that's what you want. You gotta know what she wants when she doesn't even know what she wants, you understand?"

Josh nodded in agreement.

"Well." Katy stopped and thought for a moment. "I'm sayin' don't be so bullheaded! If she's what you want, then you're gonna have to wait."

Katy was dishing out the pie and coffee before they could finish the conversation. Pie was the comfort food around the McKenzie Ranch. It fixed everything. She gave Josh a healthy piece and sat back down, quietly watching him eat it and drink his coffee.

Such a fine boy, darn good looking too, I might say. I pray, Lord, you'll shine down on him. Silently she said the small prayer.

When Josh finished the large piece of peach pie, he stood up and took the small plate and coffee cup to the sink. "I better go, Momma—I need to get back to work."

"OK, son, hope what I said helped."

"It did. I love you, Momma." He kissed her on the top of her head.

"I love you too, son."

Finally, Josh was beginning to understand a little of what Deedra might be dealing with, thanks once again to Momma's wisdom. He had no idea yet what he should do or not do regarding Deedra. But, for now, if she needed time, then he was going to give her all the time she ever wanted. He decided he wouldn't bother her, or go by the Fireside. He hoped that she would come to him when she was ready, if she was ever ready. This wouldn't be easy for Josh. He hated having to wait. Josh was never born with the virtue of patience. But, he would try his best at learning.

Chapter 14

When Deedra woke again, she was feeling somewhat better than she had earlier. She decided to get up out of bed and shower and put on some clothes and make-up to make herself feel better. Going into the kitchen, she heated a bowl of soup in the microwave, then sat down to the breakfast counter and devoured it quickly.

Her mind started to wander back to Josh. His body, the scent of the man. The way he walked, the words he spoke. The sound of his voice. The look in his eyes.

The best thing she could do to keep her mind off Josh and all the questions that kept haunting her mind was to clean the house. Walking over to the stereo, she turned on a favorite rock station she hadn't heard in years, remembering that she used to love to listen to southern rock. It seemed like so many years ago since she had listened to some great music. Craig had never cared for that type of music, so she never had the stereo turned to any other station but the one he wanted.

The thought stopped her for a moment and made her wonder. *Why had she done that? Why didn't she listen to what she wanted the same way that Craig did?* It never dawned on her before this instant that there were many things she never did because Craig did not care for it.

The sounds coming from the speaker seemed to be lifting her spirits a little, reminding her of when she was a teen. It was a precious time in her life, when she was sixteen, and things were so simple and pure. She had not yet been ready to find the man of her dreams, and yet a part of her could not wait to learn about the kiss or the sex she had heard her other friends talk about.

What happened to that time? How did everything get so messed up? she questioned herself. The reflection got her off track; her mind drifted back and forth.

She certainly didn't want to have to deal with any of this, and yet, every few moments a question popped into her mind.

Craig was good for the marriage, wasn't he? He was the perfect husband, wasn't he? Wasn't I the perfect wife? I did lay his clothes out for him, he never had to question about his dinner. The house was always immaculate. I never went anywhere unless he said it was all right to go. Those words caught in her mind for a moment, and she repeated it to herself as though she didn't hear it clearly enough. *I never went anywhere unless "he" said it was all right to go. Just like I never listened to the music or television programs he didn't care for. Just like I never wore the clothes he didn't think were appropriate. Oh my God! Marcy is right.*

Deedra couldn't quite comprehend everything she was thinking, but what she did realize was that Marcy was right. *The marriage was for my security. It wasn't a partnership, not when Craig made all of the decisions.*

Being Craig's wife had taken control of her. Maybe she had put everything else on the back burner in order to make Craig happy. But maybe that was just an element of marriage? Wasn't it? Instinctively, a small part of her already knew the answers to her questions. Yet, she was still unable to fully admit them.

The inability to realize what her marriage had really been, kept her in the safe mode that she had come to know. Deedra still had the undesirable need to have the guilt and apprehension wash over her like an old friend. To totally admit that everything Marcy said was right, would allow the chips to start to fall away from the stoned wall she had built up around her. Marcy was right about too many things. Perhaps some of what Josh had said was true as well.

What was it about Josh anyway? Why the inner turmoil? What was it about him that seemed to make her want to lose control? It didn't matter anyway. *He said he would never bother me again, so I can just let it go. Forget anything ever happened.*

When the children came in from school the next day, the house was completely spotless and their mother was back to looking like her normal self. She put a nice dinner on the table that night for them, and decided that afterwards she would sit down with the children and talk to them about their father, her life, their life and maybe even a bit about Josh as well. Throughout the day, Deedra deliberated on so many things that had occurred in her life, so many things she didn't have a full understanding over. But one factor she did realize, it was time to sit with the children and talk about their future.

With the girls bathed and sitting next to their mother on the couch, Deedra slowly moved into the conversation, easing in by first asking about school and friends.

Then, taking in a deep breath and exhaling slowly, she started a new conversation about their father, carefully, trying to speak to them in terms they would best understand. Deedra told the small children before her how much she missed their daddy. The children listened intently to their mother, telling her they missed him as well. They wished that he were still with them, but they had come to understand that it would never happen.

Cautiously, she eased her way in to the conversation about getting on with her own life. She asked if it would be OK with them if she started to go out once in a while.

Deedra had an expression of astonishment across her face. She was absolutely amazed at how well the children were responding. Everything she spoke of, they nodded in agreement. She expected them to reply with something negative about her "going out," but they didn't. Deedra started to relax a bit as the conversation seemed to move in to a less-strained atmosphere.

"What about Mr. Josh?" Jessica questioned.

"What do you mean?" Deedra asked, taken aback.

"Well, when will you see him again? I mean, I like him, Mommy, I want to go to his house again."

Casey chimed in, "Yeah, me too! I like the horses and the dogs he has. And—"

Jessica made a scrunched up face at her sister. "You always like the dogs, Casey! But, I like it all, it's really cool there, and, well, I like Mr. Josh too."

"Na-uh, Jessicaaa," Casey bickered back. "I like it all too! So there!"

"Casey, you're just saying that 'cause I did."

"OK, girls, no need to argue." Deedra busted in to the little squabble, shaking her head at them.

"Well, Mommy, she's just copying me."

"No I'm not."

"Girls!" She raised her voice a bit and gave them the "look" that told them, enough is enough.

For a moment, there was silence as both girls stared at each other, secretly wishing they could say more, but knowing that if they did the conversation would be over and they would have to go to bed.

"Mom? What about Mr. Josh, you going to date him?" Jessica asked innocently.

Deedra sat there shocked by what she had been asked. "I don't know, girls, I hadn't really thought about Mr. Josh," Deedra fibbed.

"Well, I have!" Jessica stated. "I told Casey he was gonna be our next Daddy! He is, huh?"

"What? What did you say?" A look of disbelief crossed her face, and the tone of her voice indicated she was irritated.

"Ummm, nothing, Mommy, I'm sorry."

Immediately Deedra realized her voice sounded upset. "Oh no, I'm not upset, Jessica, it just stunned me. I just never thought in a million years you would think about…another Daddy, that's all."

"Well, Mommy…" Jessica began sounding much older than the sweet child Deedra was accustomed too. "I have friends that their Daddys left them, and their Mommys got a new daddy. I tell them my daddy didn't leave; he had to go to heaven. So, well, I was thinking maybe one day me and Casey would get a new daddy."

Casey nodded her head.

Deedra was absolutely surprised. She was devoid of words to speak. Jessica had punched her mother hard in the chest, without realizing what she had done, as if hitting with her fist instead of words. The children had already let go of their father, understanding that he was not coming back, and they were willing to learn to love someone else in his place.

Apparently, she was the only one in the small group still holding on. She could not believe how intelligent and perceptive her children were. Apparently they were a lot more gifted in that department than she was.

Lying in bed that night, she felt a sense of relief come over her. It was a comfort somehow that her children, her young beautiful girls, could understand so much. She wondered if maybe now would be a good time to sell the Fireside. It was time to start being with the children more. Now was a good time to make a fresh start. Maybe invest in property.

It was time to learn how to let go of the past. The past that haunted her. She thrived on the guilt she lived with, hiding from the truth somehow. For the first time in her life, lying there quietly, she allowed the thoughts and the questions to come in to her mind and, instead of blocking them out or blowing them off as if they never existed, she tried to understand and find the answers.

Did I marry Craig because I was afraid or lonely? In many ways, he was like a father to me. I never went against any of his wishes, never questioned what he thought was best for us. Why didn't I question? Isn't that what a marriage is about? Compromise? There was no compromise, was there? I just naturally did whatever made him happy.

Craig kept her safe and warm. She never wanted for anything. There was no passion, no fire in the marriage. In fact, many of the things Josh had done with her body the other day, had never occurred to her prior to that. Craig would never have "touched" her with his mouth between her legs. She never questioned why he didn't. Mostly because she was afraid to ask, and also because she didn't really know what she needed. Perhaps because what she never had, she could not miss. But the truth was, many things in the marriage didn't feel marriage-like.

She really was not independent—never had been. Her parents had kept her safe. When they had died so tragically, Craig was there, like the knight in shining armor. He filled the empty void. She had never learned how to become independent or self-reliant. There were no chances to learn. Craig took care of everything financial. He took care of anything having to do with the household bills. The house was built in the posh neighborhood of his choosing. It was his decision that they would only have two children. He had decided what school was best for them to attend.

So, with Craig's death, the safe haven had left as well. She hid behind the walls that she had built to stay protected from feeling pain ever again. However, in doing so, she had allowed herself to be a part of the pain. It washed over her like some kind of anointment. The extra baggage she carried with her was much too heavy to carry on her shoulders. If she were to release herself from the past, she would have to learn what true independence was. To learn true independence meant taking risk in life, and she had no idea how to begin allowing those risks.

That afternoon, out at Josh's property, she felt for the first time what wanting something—desiring something—felt like. He had given her the first major orgasm she ever felt. It was a magical experience. Her body had been on fire in a way that it never before had been. Her mind had blocked all the guilt of her past out and only allowed for the fiery touches of his hands and the wanton feelings to enter and control her.

Despite the fact that Deedra didn't believe Josh fit in to her future, she could not let herself blame him for what happened. She had wanted it just as much.

But, he was a fleeting moment, something that had taken her by surprise, probably out of her loneliness. He must have come at the right moment when she was at the lowest point. So, even though she was unable to turn back the clock, she would make sure the mistake would never be repeated.

When the time was right, when she had the ability to totally let go of the past, she might consider dating then. But, there was much work to be done. Now was the time to learn independence, freedom and challenge. In spite of the willingness to change, she wondered silently if she would ever find out what love truly was. Her last thought for the night was that when tomorrow came, there was somewhere in particular she needed to go, someone important she needed to see.

The walk up the long concrete pathway lined with bright red flowering Hibiscus reminded her of a time not so long ago: the dreaded walk that took Craig's casket to its resting place. In burying Craig, the memories had come back full force of her parents' burial. The images were always fresh in her mind. The visits never got easier; they would re-open all the old wounds each time. The pain always seemed to be so close and thick in her heart.

Stopping in front of a large marble stone marker, she went down to her knees. Deedra let her fingers touch the deep engravings that marked the stone. She read the epitaph out loud to herself.

"CRAIG DAVID MARLAN, 1948-2000. Loving father, loving husband."

She let her fingers touch the deeply carpeted grass lying around the beautiful stone, then rearranged the flowers that she had delivered monthly to his gravesite by the flower shop.

"Craig," she whispered as if he could hear, "I had to come here and talk to you. I'm not sure why. I'm not sure why I'm doing this. I just know I had to come." The tears began falling lightly down her cheeks. Her voice cracked up too much to continue speaking. Only the thoughts she wanted him to hear remained.

I wish you could tell me what the right thing to do is. I tried to stay faithful to you. I tried to keep you close to my heart. Damn it, Craig, it was so simple when you were here! Why did you leave me? If you hadn't left me, none of this would have happened.

Suddenly her thoughts went silent, so silent that she could hear the small Blue jay singing off somewhere out of sight. She sat herself down Indian-style on the grass and stared off into the sunlight for what seemed like hours. She thought of all the memories of her childhood, of her desperate attempts at being different from her parents. How she had loathed the way she dressed, the way she looked. Even then she had tried changing who she was to please others. She had never been comfortable in her own skin. She was always striving to be more than her family was. She felt ashamed. So young, so immature.

Just when she was beginning to understand what life was about, her parents' sudden death had sent her spiraling out of control. Craig was the salvation from the fear and pain, the security blanket she needed to survive the multiple loss. The guilt started then. She believed that because she never truly wanted to be like her family, because she had never found pride in who they were, she somehow deserved to have lost them.

Through her innocence and lack of self-worth, Craig had come along, saving her from herself. He had married her because she was a young, innocent, sweet child that he could mold the way he wanted to. She had been a token—a possession. As wrong as she was for her actions, Craig was equally at fault.

With Craig's death, she lost the only security she had, and so she forced herself to hide from emotionally bonding with anyone. Not just his death but also his life. She had been so caught up in hiding and having someone else be responsible for her that she had never questioned what she needed in life. She never questioned her sexual life with Craig because it really did not matter. She now realized that she had never connected emotionally with him in the first place. She had been more like a robot than a woman. The words Marcy had said about "dying a slow death" were actually true. All too true!

I am so sorry, Craig. You're gone and I am sorry for that. But, I was wrong. I never should have married you just to feel safe. You should have never married me just to own me either! The words were flowing without restraint, a bit angry, but for the first time honest. *I have to stand on my own. I don't know how. But, I have to. I'm sorry, Craig, sorry for everything.*

Chapter 15

Josh tried unproductively to call Deedra at the Fireside throughout the day. Each time he called, he was told she was not there yet. They were not sure she was going to come in today. Lately, she had been keeping rather odd hours, coming in when she wanted to.

He had promised himself he would stay away from her, but he just wanted to hear her voice for a moment. It had been well over a month since he last spoken to her. Each day was harder to face. The nights seemed to be getting longer for him as well. There were times he ached to get just a glimpse of her, if only for a second—a chance encounter at the local grocery store, see her driving down the highway. Something, anything. The fantasies he had of her during the night only added to the ache.

Sometimes the anger would strike so hard that he would contemplate getting in the truck, driving to town and finding her. Just take her, take what he believed should be his. He wanted to make her love him, want him. Afterward, as the anger subsided, he would think better of acting like a fool. He knew that if he pushed too hard, she would close the doors between them forever. So one more day would pass.

Several times, in his attempt to forget Deedra existed, he went to the local bar to find a warm body to hold. He scored with two different women, twice with a blonde that had no direction in her life and once with a redhead that questioned him more about his employment capabilities than anything else. He was demanding and domineering, and he easily talked each into virtually every position he commanded of their bodies, taking his frustrations over Deedra out on them. Each of them were easily impressed. Neither one were taken to his home. Instead, he took them to the nearest hotel down the block. Unfortunately, the only thought he had when driving them home after their night of pleasure was *Why couldn't they have been Deedra...*

He had told her he would find other women, and he did. He had told her he didn't need her. It was true that he could walk in the bar and take a woman home that night, he had proved it to himself. But, nothing he did washed away the thoughts of Deedra in his mind. Thoughts of her naked body. Thoughts of her cruel words. Thoughts!

So, even though he promised her he would never bother her again—he lied. All he could think about was the woman he could not let get away.

Today he had to hear her voice. He had to be able to see her. Even if it meant she would tell him to leave her alone. The ache had become too great. When he couldn't get her by phone, he made the decision to drive to town and find her. *Even if I get kicked to the curb, it will have been worth it*, he figured.

Arriving home after the day on the town shopping with her girls, she saw Josh's truck sitting in her driveway as she pulled in. As soon as he saw it was her car, he eased out of the driver's door. Deedra looked at her watch. *Seven-thirty at night. What does he want?* The trepidation leapt up in her throat, a large lump that just wouldn't go down.

She didn't want an argument to ensue over why he was there, and why he shouldn't be. Especially in front of the children. Nevertheless, the sight of him had her nervous and apprehensive. Her stomach was twirling and her heart pounding. The same feelings she thought would have gone away in time were still quite evident. In the past several months she begged for the thoughts of him to leave her alone, especially deep in the night when her mind would play its wicked games. But, no matter how hard she forced herself to forget his existence, get on with her life without his face popping in to her mind, he just wouldn't leave her be.

Josh started adding disclaimers before he even reached her car. "Hey, look, before you throw me off your property, I just wanted to see if you were all right, and to tell you I'm sorry about the last time I saw you."

"It's OK, don't be concerned about it." She made her voice sound as though it were cold and unfeeling, hoping this would dismay him.

Josh swallowed hard. He couldn't help but feel the coldness and see the dark eyes looking directly at him. He was unable to see an ounce of expression behind them. He thought of turning and leaving without another word spoken. But, something inside of him just couldn't.

"Mr. Josh, hi!" Jessica squealed. "Are you here to see us?"

Casey ran over, grabbing his hand in hers. "Where've you been? We didn't get to come to see you."

"I've missed you girls too! Have you been good for your mommy?" he asked, raising his head up from the children, making direct eye contact again with Deedra.

"Uh huh, we were so good, Mommy took us shopping!" Jessica answered proudly.

"Jessica? How about you and your sister opening the door for me, please? I will be right in," their mother stated quietly, not really wanting them to be so chummy with Josh.

"Do you think I could come in for a few minutes, Deedra? I promise I won't stay long."

She thought about it for a second, looking toward the door where the children were, then back over to him. "Alright, but just for a little bit, OK?"

Josh raised his hand to his heart and crossed it, subsequently following her and the children into the house.

The girls were excited to see him. They were trying to tell him everything they had seen or done within the last several weeks. Deedra ushered them up the stairs to bed, telling Josh she would be back as soon as she had them settled.

Trying to kill time in the large living room, he sat down on the sofa.

He let his eyes wander around the familiarity of the large home, trying to be patient until Deedra came back from tucking the girls in. He never thought he would be here again, and he was a bit surprised that he was. He never thought he would ever come back. He told her he would never be back.

"Do you want some tea or something?" Deedra broke the silence in the room.

"Yeah, iced tea would be great if you've got it." He stood up from the couch to help her, following her to the kitchen.

"How have you been, Deedra?" Josh asked anxiously, trying to make idle conversation. For the moment, he was happy that she was speaking to him.

"I've been fine. And you?" she replied nervously.

"I'm doin' OK."

"Well, that's good."

Small talked filled the air around them. Josh talked anxiously about the new calves that had been born in the past week, but Deedra wasn't really listening; she was caught up in the tea she was pouring. Suddenly out of nowhere she wondered how tall he was. He seemed to dwarf her by so much in height.

Without warning the thoughts turned to words. "How tall are you anyway?" *God, why did I just ask that?*

"I'm six foot four! What about you?"

"Oh, I'm five foot on the nose."

Josh broke out into laughter.

"What's so funny?" she asked, not really understanding why he was laughing.

"Oh, nothing really! Just, well, you're like a china doll. You know, small. Kinda like a little Pixie."

"Oh, OK." Deedra looked up at him, smiling slightly, remembering how beautiful his large eyes were when he smiled, and the fine lines that kissed the sides of his eyes. Without being conscious of it she was staring at them, mesmerized by the twinkling effect they seemed to have.

Misunderstanding the look, Josh bent down and kissed her.

She jerked away from him immediately, slapping him hard across the left side of his face. Instantaneously she was regretful of her involuntary reaction.

He stood there glaring, the sensation of the sting burning his cheek.

Instinctively, Deedra reached for his face, attempting to touch the reddened area. "I'm so sorry, I just overreacted!" she said, trying her best to apologize. "You were just supposed to come in for a few minutes, Josh, not do this!"

It did infuriate her in fact. He should not have taken it upon himself to kiss her like that. She was on guard against him anyway, still threatened by the fear of him of him being too close.

He stood there in stony silence, staring at her, his eyes filled with pain of wanting something so badly it hurt. When her hand touched his face, he backed himself away from her, standing there motionless. His jaw was rigid, his teeth clenched.

"I really am sorry, Josh! I said I was sorry, I didn't mean to hurt you." Cautiously, she reached up again to touch him. Only this time, he grabbed her hand, pushing it away with a swift movement.

"Well, say something then!" she implored. "Don't just stand there, say something!"

If that's what you want, I will damn sure say something! he thought in the midst of his fury. Josh grabbed for her, quickly bringing her to him, putting one hand around the back of her neck. Without so much as a word, he kissed her hard.

She gasped for air and tried to free herself, but his grasp on her was uncompromising. She felt fear deep in the core of her being. His mouth was hard and demanding, threatening to bruise her lips from the pressure. The kiss was fiery, intense, scorching and volatile. She detested both him and herself for feeling her nipples come alive from his kiss.

As briskly as he had grabbed her, he let her go. Her legs felt weak, and she thought she might fall. Deedra slapped at him again, this time meaning to hit him as hard as she possibly could, but was unable to make contact.

She had apologized for the slap earlier, he knew she didn't want him to kiss her, and yet he had done it anyway. She could not allow him to gain the upper hand. *How dare he think he can just do this to me ...*

"Who the hell do you think you are? You can't just kiss someone and expect them to respond! Damn you! What is wrong with you!" Her tone indignant and extremely enraged.

Josh clenched his teeth, letting the hot flush of ferocity urge him on like a powerful drug. He grabbed for her, kissing her again. Only this time he didn't release her face right away. He stood there staring into her eyes, daring her to slap him.

"Hit me again, Deedra! Come on, I'm waiting, hit me again," Josh whispered irately, egging her on. His mouth was only inches from hers.

She tried to slap him again, as he had dared her to. Yet, once again, he caught her hand, putting it down behind her back and holding it tightly there. Positioning his right arm down to the small of her back, he lifted her up to make her almost as tall as he was, then pushed her back against the refrigerator door.

Holding her forcefully against the refrigerator with his weight, he kissed and tongued whatever his mouth could reach of her face and neck. "Hit me, damn it! Go ahead, hit me!" he repeatedly hissed in between the hard-pressed kisses, knowing full well that she could not strike him from the position she was in.

"Hit me, Deedra! Come on, I'm waiting!"

Josh had his body pressed so tightly against her she was having a hard time taking in air. A part of her was so terrified—terrified of what he was going to do to her. Yet, her body was fighting against her as well, burning with desire for him to continue.

"God I hate you! I detest you!" she said breathlessly. "You're nothing more than an ogre, a beast! I hate you so much!" she snarled. "God, I hate you!" she repeated. She was so angry at him for doing this to her, but also angry at herself for wanting him to do it.

Coming back to his senses, Josh realized what he was doing. Shaking his head in absolute disgust with himself for what he was doing, he quickly let go of her, and her body slid down the face of the refrigerator and back to a standing position.

Deedra was lightheaded, leaning back against the appliance door for support. In a flash of a second, he turned, walking out of the kitchen without a word. Deedra was walking behind him, almost at his heels.

"I can't believe I did this!" he said, shaking his head as he walked. "Gawd, I can't believe this!" he declared apprehensively, continuing toward the front door. "I'm so sorry—so very sorry I came here, honest to Gawd, all I wanted—I just wanted to see if you were OK. I get around you and I just don't have common sense, I guess."

She was listening to his every word, following him to the door. When he reached for the door, he stopped to take one last look at her, knowing this would be the last time he would ever see her face. He was sickened with himself even more when he saw her tear-stained face.

"I promise you, I won't ever come back! I won't ever do this to you again!" He was so ashamed that he had acted in such a manner. Never in his life had he ever done anything so cruel. He opened the door and started out.

Her heart fell to the floor. She couldn't understand why either. She didn't understand her need to have him do whatever he wanted to her body, or why she would be angry when he would. Everything seemed so overwhelming, she began sobbing uncontrollably.

He turned back toward her, feeling an overwhelming guilt for causing this. A thin stream of tears became obvious on his own cheeks. No one could have been more shocked than Josh—he was never the type of man to shed tears.

"Deedra, I never meant to hurt you, I swear to Gawd! I know you will never ever believe that." He wanted to go to her and hold her, but he knew it would never be allowed. He had to recognize the awful truth—she did not want him, and after today, there would be no more chances. Rather than to continue hurting her, he would leave and never bother her again.

"Josh, no! I mean—wait, please!" she begged, loud enough for him to hear through the closing door.

"What?" he asked, as if only imagining her words.

"I don't know what…I don't know why, I just can't let you go," she stammered. "Not yet! Oh my God, what is wrong with me?" she asked, as if she was asking Josh to tell her.

"Deedra? What are you saying?"

"I don't know, I just don't know."

She walked over to him hesitantly, reaching up for his neck, softly bending his head down to meet hers. She let her lips touch the tear-stained cheek, tasting the salt against her lips.

He picked his head back up from her. " I don't know what you want, Deedra."

"I wish I knew, wish I knew!" she repeated. She was still confused at the fact of her telling him not to go. The words were reeling in her head. There were no answers. It would have been so much easier to let him walk out the door. Nonetheless, the feeling in her chest, the heaviness of her heart, was begging to make him stay.

"Talk to me, Deedra, please?"

"I don't know. I mean, all I can say is, I feel odd! Like, if you leave right now, I will never be the same again."

"You didn't call me or anything during this whole time. I was left wondering, just wishing I could hear your voice or see you for a minute, something. Then when I see you, I act stupid! I'm just runnin' in circles here, I think."

"I know, I feel like that too, and I don't know why," she interrupted.

"Yeah, well, I'm goin' crazy, that's all I know! I wish just once you would tell me what you really want!" Josh countered. "I made a mistake in there," he said, pointing toward the kitchen. "I thought I saw something in your eyes that wasn't there, and I kissed you—Big Mistake! Then I lose my mind, and it's because of you."

"Why me?"

"I don't know, Deedra; I guess I see things in your eyes that aren't really there. I do stupid crap and get slapped for it! I kiss you and you slap me, I try to leave and you tell me not to! I am really confused by you!"

"I don't know what I want, I'm not sure what I need!" she interjected, wiping the tears from her face with her hand.

"I really wished I could have had the chance to show you who I really am! I'm not an evil monster, even if I do act like it sometimes. I just look like I am because I ache to be with you!"

Deedra stood there before him, silent. She had no idea what she should say, had no idea how to tell a man how she felt. She couldn't remember ever telling Craig what her emotions were. There were no heartfelt talks between them. This was uncharted territory for her.

"I do want you, Josh, I just don't know why yet, but I do! I'm just—I don't know, I guess scared." Her voice broke to a whisper. She was petrified of trying to tell him her thoughts, as well as being hesitant about how to actually go about it. How could she begin to tell him that a mature woman with children, with a marriage under her belt, had no idea how to relate to, share feelings with or tell her thoughts to a man?

Josh stopped in his tracks and turned to look at her, interrupting her words, "Then tell me what you want! You have to tell me!" he said, slapping his right hand against the middle of his chest.

"I don't know what you want me to say?" she responded.

"Look, baby, you got to say something! Do you feel anything for me?"

"I think so…"

"What do you feel then, answer that."

"I'm not sure, Josh, I know it seems silly, but I don't know—"

"Either you want to try or you don't! It's that simple."

"No it's not simple!" she answered defensively. "I really don't know, Josh! I'm being honest; I don't know what it is I want, I just—just couldn't let you walk out the door."

"Then try being honest with yourself for once, Deedra, that would be a start," he remarked. "Do you or don't you have feelings for me? That's the question!"

"Yes, I think so, but—"

"You think so? You don't know? Was it a huge mistake, the day at the ranch I mean?"

"Not a mistake, Josh, I wanted it too, I wanted you," she answered, wishing she knew the right words to make him understand.

"For what? A quick roll in the hay?" His voice was rising a little.

"Is that all it was, Deedra? Answer that!"

"No, I wanted you. I didn't know it, but I did!" she screamed out, then realized how loud she sounded, and she was afraid she might wake the children.

"What did you want me for? A pansy? Someone you'll see if you ever make a decision that you want to? What do you want *me* for?"

"No, Josh, No! Oh hell, I don't know."

Without a sound, Deedra walked over to him, laying her body against him and wrapping one arm around his waist. She reached to touch his face, to reach his lips.

"Josh, please, I don't know! I don't know what to say. All I know is I don't want you to leave. I don't know why, but I feel this odd feeling in my stomach. Josh—just please kiss me."

Those words stunned Josh; he had been slapped twice earlier for doing just that. He bent down to her, kissing her tenderly, yet guardedly.

"No, Josh, I mean…I want you to kiss me."

Without forethought or malice, he did not kiss her this time. Instead, he picked her up in his arms, cradling her close to him as if she were some tiny rag doll and carried her to her bedroom.

A shiver ran up her spine. For the first time, she laid herself close to him and let herself be carried. The only thing she was certain of at this moment was that she did not want him to leave, and she really needed to be with him tonight.

Entering the bedroom, he turned with her still in his arms and shut the door with his foot. Walking her over to the bed, he stood her up on the mattress, making her virtually face to face with him.

"Now show me what you want, baby, 'cause I'm not gonna make another wrong move with you."

Apprehensively she touched his face in her small soft hands, gently putting her lips to his. Softly she kissed his lips, the corners and the center. She let her shaking hands run through his long silky hair as she did. She had never been the aggressor in bed, having no idea what she was supposed to do to please a man. Surely she had never initiated sex with a man. Craig had never allowed the time to learn. She would just lie there and let him use her body for his pleasure.

Now with Josh, she had no idea how to relate to him the things going through her mind. She was not sure what she should do to show him or how she was supposed to please him. For now, she would continue to gently kiss his lips, his eyes and his cheeks. She backed away from him, her hands trembling so badly that she was having difficulty unbuttoning her blouse.

Josh grabbed for her hands, and with his hands over hers he took the silky fabric between their hands and ripped it away from her, letting the buttons fall where they may on the floor, exposing her bare breasts to him.

Deedra's lungs let out a gasp of air at the ferocious removal of the article of clothing. Her heart quickened from the feeling. Josh put his hands back down to holding either side of her waist as if he had never done anything at all.

Her breasts, exposed and lying against Josh's shirt, made her feel wanton. She continued to run her hands through his hair, kissing at his lips, neck and forehead. She was trembling uncontrollably, having a hard time standing firmly on her feet, begging for air to enter her aching hot body.

Josh was losing patience waiting for her to do more, so he decided to take the initiative. He let his hands slowly slide down the sides of her body to the bottom of her skirt, allowing his hands to slide up her leg and to the back of her hips. Grabbing at the tiny lace panties, he pushed the silky material down to expose her full round buttocks. Cupping the cheeks of her rear in each of his massive hands, he firmly forced her body closer to his.

She continued to kiss his face. She wanted him so badly and yet she had no idea how to tell him what she wanted. She was trying not to think, just feel her way from his face to his neck and then to his chest. She liked feeling the muscles as they tensed underneath the black t-shirt. She reached for the bottom of the shirt and brought it up over his head, exposing his dark gleaming skin. For a moment she stopped to look in his eyes, watch the twinkling effects that they had. The little crystals of light danced within them.

Pushing her breasts against his hot skin caused a low groan to escape his lips, and she allowed her hands to move slowly over his arms, finding any areas she could reach with her touch. No words came from her mouth, no aggressive moves on her part. She was like a young girl that was beginning her very first experience with a man.

Josh felt her trembling, could hear her heart beating hard against him. He could feel the awkward touches and kisses to his skin.

Finally, it dawned on him; she had no idea how to make love with a man. She had no idea what she was doing, or what steps to take. *Oh my Gawd!* Did this girl live in a bubble somewhere? She was married, how could she not know? *Yet, she has no clue what she is doing. She doesn't know! Oh my Gawd, she doesn't know.*

Without words to express what he finally understood, he took over the controls and began undressing her like a pro, masterfully pulling her skirt and panties down with one swift movement.

In a matter of seconds, she was standing before him naked. Picking her up in a fireman's carry, he laid her down in the middle of the bed and then positioned himself beside her. He let his hands massage the beautiful round breast, positioning her so that he could gain access to each of her nipples equally. Slowly he sucked, then let his tongue swirl around the hardened nipple, then he would suck again. Moving his hand down the line of her belly, he let his fingers slide between her legs, inserting his index and middle fingers deep inside of her. She was already extremely wet. He knew what she wanted, could hear it in the low groans in her throat; it brought a smirk to his face. Slowly he let the fingers slide in and out of her silkened wetness. Without forewarning her, he pushed both fingers forward inside her, as if pushing toward her belly, sending her into an instantaneous orgasm.

With the first orgasm out of the way, he knew that she would be open and responsive to his touch. Now he could slow down a bit and let her enjoy the sensations. If she had never been with a man that had given her pleasure, tonight she would. Tonight he would make her body feel things that her mind would not even comprehend. He watched her eyes flicker, loved the mystical look they gave him with each wondrous phenomenon he produced for her pleasure. He watched the unique expressions as he let his fingers go in and out of her slowly, taking her to the edge, stopping and then to the edge again. He watched as her back arched, anticipating the moment of ecstasy. Then just as the moment was close to arrival, he would stop, wait for her body to calm, kiss her passionately, then start the process over again.

"Make love to me, Josh," she cried out.

"Oh no, baby, I'm going to do everything else to you but make love," he growled.

A strange look came over her face, not understanding what he meant.

"When you can accept the fact that I do love you, we will make love! Until then, I do it my way."

Slowly and methodically, he was driving her mad with desire. He was taking great pleasure in controlling her body, the look in her eyes, the way the sounds came out of her partly opened lips. She was his; she had to be his. His to use, his for this moment in time— his pleasure. When he was sure she had enough, he stood up and over her on the bed and removed his clothing. Without a word, he came back down over her, entered her and, moving his hips intensely and fast, rigidly thrust into her , hard, deeply and powerfully.

It no longer mattered if she had a release. This was his. This is what he wanted. To be deep within her. Her hot wetness consumed him, making his muscles feel as though they were on fire. At the moment of release, he brought his mouth over hers to contain his own scream.

Chapter 16

Josh rolled over to get closer to where Deedra was lying, taking her up in his arms, gently kissing her lips. The beast that was there earlier, hard and unyielding, was all but gone, replaced by this softer, gentler man.

"My sweet baby," his voice cooed soft and tender. "I wish you could realize you're everything I could ever want."

"You don't know me, Josh, you don't know me at all," she murmured, her voice tired.

"I know more than you realize, girl, a lot more than you give me credit for."

For the first time, Deedra opened herself up to a man, to Josh. She explained her past, the death of her parents, the marriage to Craig and the spiraling effect that she seemed to have been caught in even before her parents' untimely death. She was open and candid about her lack of abilities in the bed and why, finding the words of honesty in telling him her first major orgasm was when they were out in the pasture.

Josh was able to understand the inabilities she had in bed, understood the inability to perform earlier; she would need guidance to learn. In spite of this, he just never imagined that she was the novice that she was. If it had not been for the fact that she had a sexual history and had given birth, her lack of skills would have led him to believe that she was still a virgin.

It made him feel sadness for her. She had all the wealth one could ever hope for, but she was lacking in what mattered most in life; love, passion and intrigue. Josh lifted her up, cradling her in his arms for a moment, then lay her gently back on the bed.

Getting up, Josh looked over toward her. "I'd better go now." He really didn't want to leave her, but he didn't want the children to get the wrong idea.

Deedra watched him as he stood up from the bed. For the first time, she actually was looking at all of him naked before her. He was the most beautifully built man she had ever seen. His body glistened a golden color with the deep richness of his tanned skin. The muscles in his legs, his arms, and his stomach rippled. His incredible manhood was large and thick, lying dormant now to the right of his rock-hard thigh.

"Don't leave me, Josh, not yet." Her voice broke. She was amazed that for once, she had made a decision. She really did want him to stay. She was also realizing that the time she was away from him, all she did was think of why they should not be together. He never left her mind.

Josh turned back toward the bed and sat down. "I'll stay as long as you want." He smiled at her and pulled the sheet and comforter down to expose her body. He lay down next to her, delicately touching her breast, barely a whisper of contact. He let his fingers encircle the areola around her rock-hard nipples.

Deedra closed her eyes, a sigh escaping her lips. She believed that yet again he would ravish her body, and she knew she would let him.

"Go to sleep, Sunshine, I will be here when you wake up."

I don't understand his signals at all, she thought to herself as sleep claimed her.

Deedra woke to the ache of wanting. Josh had been softly caressing her as she slept, waking her body to the feelings of him touching her sides and that of her lower back. Gently he was manipulating the skin under his fingertips. He didn't have to see her body in the daylight to know how completely fascinating it was. He could feel with his hands the small, round fullness of her rear, the slight curves of her hips. She was not a svelte little thing like a model. He felt her tummy; it was not completely flat and muscular like so many women he had been with. It had this unique softness to it as well, a plumpness. It was a perfect little tummy, exactly what he thought a real woman should look like.

"What time is it?" she asked in her sleepy haze.

"It's three a.m.," he answered quietly.

She turned over toward him to face him on the bed, letting him continue to move his hands across her body. Even without fully being awake, Deedra could smell the scent of sex from earlier, an extraordinary, intoxicating aroma. Taking in a slow deep breath, she let the smell fill up her senses. It aroused her, even more than the touches were doing.

He could not get enough of the soft skin or the paleness of it in the moonlight against his deeply tanned skin. The thought of the contrast between the two of them was so sinfully erotic to him. Feeling her skin dance from the tickling sensation, he leaned into her and kissed her tenderly, searching her lips, her mouth, playing with her lips with his tongue.

This was a unique and wickedly sweet feeling, like so many of the new feelings she was experiencing with him. She really did not know this tower of a man that was lying in her bed. They had never formally dated, never really divulged all of the secrets of their lives. Yet, something happened last night. Something exquisite.

She wanted him to touch her, caress her. She needed his lips on her, devouring every part of her being. The feelings he gave her body were unmatched by anything she had ever known. She just couldn't seem to get enough. She also liked him taking control, taking from her what he wanted.

"Love me, Josh, please, I want you to make love to me!" she begged softly.

Her body reunited by the fire in his fingertips. She became conscious to the reality that he did control her to some extent. He had that gift. Even at her angriest, his touch seemed to transform her into another being, someone sexy, wanting and so desirable. It was as if the more powerful the act itself was, the more she craved having it. Even when he was angry and fierce, like earlier in the kitchen, all her mind could think of was how much she desired him, only making her want him more.

He did not answer her pleadings. Instead, he was silent and daunting. In the silence of the night, only a flicker of light to distinguish the two bodies, he let his fingers control her body to his liking. He was tormenting her playfully. He moved his head down to between her legs, raising her legs up and positioning them wide apart. His tongue searched out the core of her desire. The sweetness of the taste and texture was exhilarating. The taste of the both of them was still fresh from just a few hours before.

He was manipulating, teasing the soft flesh, listening carefully to the sounds she was making. He encircled his tongue around the little button. Slowly he let his tongue lick at the softness, the sweet taste on his lips. He listened, enjoying her soft moans. He slowly inserted his finger, once again without warning, and pushed forward, hitting her G-spot; she could hear a devilish laugh heard in the distance when she exploded.

She was aching, her whole body throbbing with the beat of her heart. He repeated the process again, taking her over the edge. Every once in a while he would stop just as she urged for more, and lightly lick at the swollen area. Then he would rub the small button between his teeth and initiate the process over again. He did not need to see her face to know the expressions on it. He could feel it with the pressure of her hands holding his head tightly against her.

He watched the transformation take place before his eyes. Deedra's inhibitions and lack of awareness about her body washed away with the early morning light. Her hips were meeting up to the thrust of his fingers, his tongue, and his teeth against her. She was begging for more. Anything, everything.

When he was sure she was at the fieriest level of emotional heights he could take her to, he entered her fiercely, like that of an animal. He held tightly to her arms, bringing her legs up so that her calves were next to his head. He wanted deep penetration. He heard her scream out from the desire. The heat was so intense, her skin felt on fire. He watched, he listened; he slowly and methodically pushed himself in and out of her until his body exploded with hers.

When morning came, bringing Deedra out of her deep slumber, Josh was gone. She lay there for what seemed like an hour, slowly touching her body where he had been. Her body was exhausted, yet it tingled everywhere that she touched. Getting up from the bed, she slowly made her way to the mirror. Touching her breasts and stomach, she remembered the feelings that had been stimulated within her earlier. His touch was still there. His taste was on her skin. His smell, that intoxicating aroma she had only dreamed of before, truly was apart of her bedroom now. It was so glorious.

It was implausible that she had gone most of her life not having those magnificent feelings. Nothing had ever awakened her body the way Josh could.

Chapter 17

Still reeling from Josh's touch, she went into the bathroom and started a tub of hot water, mixing the wonderful liquid Gardenia she enjoyed so much in the water. Slowly she eased herself in until her body was able to withstand the water's temperature.

With her legs out straight, she splashed the hot water all over, then eased back to begin the relaxation of her tired muscles, letting the bubbles move over her arms, breasts, and stomach. The feeling of pleasure warmed her and she laid her head back against the rim of the tub and closed her eyes. It was not long before she began imagining the soap bubbles were Josh's hands caressing her arms, stomach, breasts and legs. Slowly she traced the contours of her curves. It felt deliciously sinful.

Finally, she wondered how much time had passed, deciding it was time to stop daydreaming and rinse herself off. With the running water from the tap, she gave herself a better rinsing and then quickly washed her hair. Stepping out of the tub, she blanketed her warm body with a towel, wrapping the second one around her head. For the first time in a very long time, she felt as if her body was in total relaxation. At least for the moment, the stress and anger had subsided and she felt a bit freer. The towels still wrapped around firmly around her, she climbed back in her bed and slept.

Later that evening, the phone rang. Josh asked if she would go out to dinner with him. It would be their first official date. Though it pleased Deedra to go, a part of her felt apprehensive about it as well.

She did not know why; after all, she knew Josh in an intimate way, but the fear of getting to know him on a personal level, to know the real Josh, scared her to the bone.

It took her much time to find the perfect dress to wear. She finally decided on a deep navy, velour and lace dress with a sweeping bottom. She hoped the dress looked casual enough. She was afraid to over-do her attire when she had no idea where they might be going.

Opening the door at exactly 6:30, the exact time Josh said he would arrive, she saw before her one of the most striking men she had ever seen. He was wearing a black western shirt with pearl white snaps, black jeans, black boots and one of his favorite black Stetson hats. The blackness of his hair seemed to set off the entire outfit, making him ooze with a mysterious sensuality.

Kissing her on the cheek, he complimented her, saying, "You look gorgeous, Sunshine."

"Well, if you don't mind me saying so, you look quite handsome yourself, Josh," she replied, sounding a bit shy.

"Let's get going. I know I'm starving. Are you?"

"Indeed I am!" Deedra replied. Then she offered a polite thank you when Josh opened the front door for her to walk through. After walking her over to the large black truck, he reached out and opened the door for her, then helped her up inside. When he was satisfied that she was comfortably in, he closed her door and walked around to his own side.

Anxious to know where they were going, she turned to him and asked, "Where are we going for dinner?"

"I'm taking you to this little restaurant I used to frequent. It's not anything like the Fireside, but they have good food, great drinks and friendly people. It's called The Lodge Restaurant. I really think you will enjoy their food," he answered confidently.

It did not seem as if they had been driving for very long before Josh pulled off the highway and into a parking area. As he maneuvered the big truck into a parking spot, placing them closer to the restaurant door, she noticed that the restaurant resembled that of a large cabin. Once parked, he came around to her side, took her by the hand, and helped her out. The touch of his hand sent a shiver through her spine. She had never realized before now how gentlemanly he was—respectable and thoughtful. Was he always this way with women? Or only acting this way with her?

With his hand on the small of her back, he guided her towards the restaurant. This was something she was not accustomed to. Again, she wondered if he was always this sweet. After opening the door for her to walk in first, she stepped into the foyer and waited for him to close the door behind them. While looking around, it appeared that the restaurant was not very large. It looked as if it could only seated around forty people.

While waiting to be seated, she stole a quick glance of Josh's features. *God, he is so handsome*, she considered. Interrupting her thoughts, the hostess approached them with a friendly greeting and asked if they would like a table. Returning her politeness, Josh casually suggested a table that sat in a corner, which would leave them to dine in privacy. Once seated, he did not hesitate to begin glancing over his menu selections. As he did so, she took the opportunity to steal another look at him. He had such a rugged appearance, a hard-edged looking face. His lips were so soft looking that they made her remember the softness of his kisses.

"What looks good to you?" he asked, cutting in to her thoughts.

Embarrassed by her lack of attention, she quickly looked down and began roaming her eyes over her own menu. She just knew that he had to have noticed her staring at him. Apparently, she was not quick enough, because he had flashed her that knowing smile, but acted as if he did not notice her behavior. Focusing all her attention on the menu was now a chore. She had forgotten her hunger. The menu was small, with different selections of hamburgers, sandwiches, onion rings and fries. A shrimp platter or a large salad were the dinner-type foods.

"I know this is not what you're accustomed to, Deedra, but I think you will enjoy it."

"It's fine, Josh, stop worrying. It seems very quaint."

The server introduced herself as Heather and went on to ask for their order. Looking at Deedra, Josh asked, "What would you like to drink?"

"I think a glass of white zinfandel on the rocks would be wonderful," she answered.

"Just give me a Miller Light," he answered the hostess.

While taking a sip of her wine, Deedra took a moment to look around at the lodge's décor. In the center of each table, there were condiments and candle lamps. The walls were done in tongue and groove. On a wall above one of the tables, there hung a large moose's head. There were wall lamps, spaced evenly apart, which matched the ones on all the tables. Also on the walls, neatly hung, were pictures of bears, deer, and wolves. Bringing her eyes back to Josh, she commented, "You know, this really is a cozy little place."

"I like it, used to be my favorite place," he said. "Did you know you have the most beautiful eyes, Deedra?" he stated without warning.

She became suddenly mute. He had complimented her, and yet she was not sure how to respond to it. She felt awkward and very shy. "Thank you, Josh," she said quietly.

Deedra had thought that perhaps Josh would want to stay the night after their wonderfully sweet date. She was mistaken. Acting the perfect gentleman, he brought her home, took her to the door, held her face in his hands and kissed her goodnight.

For a moment she was left wondering, then a huge smile came over her face as she stepped through the threshold of the door. He was so unexplainable. There was no way to grasp his originality, there was nothing run of the mill about him at all.

It seemed a lifetime ago since he had met Deedra. He could not remember how life could have been livable without her in it. Nearly three months had passed since that momentous early morning of love they had shared, when Deedra finally was able to release herself to him.

The differences between them were still quite prevalent. Josh wanted marriage; Deedra was balking at the very idea of it. The more he pressed for it, the more she backed away, like closing a door. She realized she loved Josh, and she was able to comprehend the fine lines between love and hate. There were no doubts left in Deedra's heart that she wanted to be with him as much as possible, but the word "marriage" scared her to the core of her being.

The lovemaking sessions were more intense each time they were together. Deedra learning numerous mind-blowing lessons about herself, lessons only imagined existed. Wonderful nights lying next to his exquisite body. The pleasure of giving of herself willingly to his demands. Even realizing she liked having a man that dominated her body like only he knew how.

However, Craig had demanded her life and her personality, choosing what was proper and improper in regards to it. Josh did not care. Whatever decision she made in her life was fine by him, but in the bedroom it was another story. There he could dominate and control. Her body was his possession. Deedra found she actually craved that side of him.

But, in spite of all of this, learning to trust him had taken a bit more time. Even though she trusted in him now, she could not bring herself to trust in marriage or what might happen after. The word in itself, no matter how important to Josh, sent a surge of foreboding through her whenever he mentioned it.

The children, all of them, were pushing just as hard. They were anxious to become a family, to be married to each other, "real brothers and sisters" in their eyes. Even Josh's mother, brother and sister-in-law were eager for it to happen, especially Katy. She knew Deedra was the perfect woman for her renegade, hard-edged son. Deedra could settle his restless spirit down, give him the family style of life he had been in search of. Katy new Josh was a difficult and sometimes unyielding man, but with a patient and loving woman, the possibilities for him were limitless.

The last few months had been a tough time for Josh aside from Deedra, which only made him want to cling to marriage and a family all the more.

Lindsey, his favorite ex, had moved on to bigger and better things in her life, namely money. She had met and married a wealthy gentleman, then decided to move out of state to his large home. She decided that she no longer wanted her sons, Darrin and Dusty, underfoot. It had been a hard pill to swallow for Josh. He could not imagine any mother that could discard her own children like that, especially his children's mother. It made him even more aware of wanting what was best for the boys, and he worried constantly what this type of change might do to them.

Josh had become overprotective, trying to keep the boys from feeling any more pain than had already been unleashed. It caused Josh to push marriage to Deedra even further. He wanted so badly to give his sons the life they deserved. They all deserved it.

There would be sacrifices on all of their parts—he knew this. Especially for Deedra and her children. They were so used to the conveniences of the city, a store on every corner. Then there was the distinction of living in a posh neighborhood of upper class influence; the children had only played and gone to school with the higher-class population. It would be difficult, especially for Deedra, to live so far away from town, out in the wooded countryside. Her children would have to go to school with the "ordinary" children that lived out on the surrounding ranches and farms of the area.

Yet, in his heart, he knew that if Deedra would consent to it, she would find the peacefulness she had been searching for in her soul and grow to love the slower pace.

There were times when Josh would get angry because of her inability to commit to him; it was making him absolutely crazy. Sometimes he wanted to forget the whole mess. He knew better, though; he could never walk away. Every time he looked into her eyes, he realized he could never live without her in his life in some manner.

Deedra was his fire, his passion for life. She made all things possible, even in impossible times. She calmed the angry beast, when no one else could. In all of his determination and tough-as-nails perseverance, Josh could be tamed and quieted by the devotion of this woman.

Deedra wanted so much to give him what he wanted. He had brought her into the world of the living. Her wonderfully bold and boisterous Knight in White Armor had the ability to unlock and release the passions within her soul. He had opened her eyes to so many things she had missed in life. She would willingly give him anything he could ever want, except marriage.

It was not that she did not want to be Josh's wife; it just held such a frightening emotion to the word. She was not really sure why it scared her so much, but it made her quiver with terror every time the subject came up. Her best friend knew why, though. Marcy was well aware of the problem. It was still Craig. Deedra had the immense fear that what had happened to Craig would happen to Josh if they were to be man and wife. The worry over it made Deedra believe it would be easier to walk away from the relationship now, rather than to suffer through the tremendous loss she would feel if something terrible happened to Josh. Marcy was smart enough to know that no matter what she believed, her friend would not trust in her words until she actually realized it herself and got past it.

The house was full of excitement, the barbeque grill billowing out the smell of meat cooking to perfection. It was Thanksgiving and Josh had decided that instead of the standard turkey meal, he wanted to throw a huge party with sauce-slathered pork cooked in the oak wood grill. Josh had invited Marcy, Brad and their children to come and enjoy the day. The large picnic area filled with the laughter of the children playing.

The men were enjoying a game of horseshoes, while the two women laughed at some of the ridiculous moves the two men made while trying to score. It brought a smile to Marcy's lips watching the expressions in Deedra's eyes, the amusement on her face. She remarked to her at how beautifully Deedra glowed. Marcy was ecstatic to see her friend this happy.

Deedra went deep in thought for a few moments as she watched everyone play. She had finally, over the course of the last couple of weeks, decided to let go of the Fireside. The time had come for her to release yet another piece of the past that belonged to Craig. Today would be the day to talk to Marcy and Brad about it. If they wanted the business, she was willing to hand it over to them lock, stock and barrel and take back a small 20 percent profit from the net proceeds it would bring in for them per year.

She did not want to sell them the business; there was no reason in her mind not to give it to them as a gift. She had never been a big spender, so a great deal of the money that Craig had left behind was still securely in place in the bank and in money market accounts, stocks and bonds. So, why not give her friends something nice to build a foundation for their future?

She decided that she would put the 20 percent profit she would get off the business into separate accounts for Jessica and Casey's future. It would be a remembrance of their father to do with as they wished when they were old enough to decide how they wanted to spend it.

Sitting at the large picnic table eating all the wonderful food before them, Deedra casually announced her wishes to them as if she was talking about something far less important than the restaurant. The look on their faces was priceless. Both Marcy and Brad were completely shocked. Neither was sure they actually heard what Deedra said. The words were too good to believe. Therefore, Deedra repeated herself.

"I want the two of you to have the Fireside, if you want it!" She smiled brightly.

"You're kidding me, right?" Marcy gasped, practically choking on the bite of potato salad she was trying to swallow.

"No, I'm not kidding! Do you?"

"You want me to just take it over?" Marcy inquired, her words shaky.

"That's what I'm asking you, Marcy, do you and Brad want the business?" she asked again.

"We have to pay something for it, Deedra. We can't just take it over," Brad spoke up, still not sure this was really happening.

"No, you don't! You can pay me twenty percent of the profit every year. I will put ten percent into each of my girls' accounts. That is all I'm asking for," Deedra responded.

"But, Deedra, still…. I mean, the building alone is worth more than what you will get from that twenty percent," he rationalized.

"Look, you two, the building and the property on it is worth over $850,000, last time it was appraised. You will net approximately $420,000 or more a year based on what was made last year. You will pay me about $84,000 a year for my percentage, that's what I want! That's *all* I want!"

Marcy sat frozen for a moment, tears streaming down her face. Then she stood up abruptly, grabbing up her friend and hugging her tightly. Brad walked over and joined in the hug as well. He was still unable to totally believe that she was just willing to hand the business over.

It was not just about the money, it was about Craig. Marcy could not believe that Deedra was just going to let go of such a huge part of Craig's life, of her life. Releasing the restaurant would be like releasing a ghost for Deedra.

Josh was stunned. It had never dawned on him that Deedra had so much money, let alone that she had a business that was worth that much or that she was willing to just walk away from it. He knew she lived in a huge house in the best part of town. He even understood that she had money by her appearance and the Lexus car that she drove. Yet, for some reason it had never dawned on him that her late husband had left her an extremely wealthy woman. Not that any of it mattered to him. He had more than enough money from the ranch to take care of her needs.

Because it was so late when Marcy and Brad left, Josh asked Deedra if she and the girls would like to stay the night rather than to take the long drive home. Deedra agreed; she wanted to talk with Josh anyway.

Josh had his own agenda. The more that Deedra and her children spent time at the ranch…the easier he thought the transition would be for them to live there full time.

Deedra returned from putting all the children down to bed. It was fun tucking all of them in, especially the boys. Each wanted her to kiss them good night. It gave her a warm feeling knowing they were comfortable with her and wanted her to be close to them.

Josh had cleaned up the mess and lit the fireplace. Deedra sat down on the rug in front of it and lay back on the large pillow lying next to her. She patted the floor next to her, motioning Josh to come and sit down. "What did you think about what I did today?" Deedra inquired of him.

"I think if that's what you want to do, then you did a good thing," he answered. "You know, I have more than enough money for the whole family to live on, without using your money."

"Josh McKenzie! You're sneaky." She giggled.

"What? What did I do?"

"You brought up marriage again!"

"How did I do that? I never said the word marriage," he said, acting coy.

"OK, well you implied it." She laughed

"Well excuse me, I'm trying to get it through your head, I guess. You're so damn contrary, you know!"

"Me? Me, contrary? Isn't that like calling the kettle black, Mr. Pot?" Deedra chuckled. "Just shut up for a minute, McKenzie, will you? I was going to have a serious talk with you, but no, you had to divert the conversation!" she said, acting as if she was upset at him.

"Oh, now that's not my fault?" He was amused at her. "All I was saying was that we would all have enough money. We won't need to use any of yours."

"Um, Josh?" She looked over at him, still smiling from their pretend fight.

"Yes?"

"Get over here and kiss me," she insisted.

"Only if I get to start at your pretty lil toes and work my way up." He winked.

"You always get your way, don't you?" she purred.

"Yeah, I do!" He smiled sheepishly. "Well, most of the time."

"Stop talking and get over here to me." She extended her foot toward him.

Chapter 18

Wednesday morning of the following week, Deedra woke out of a deep slumber deathly sick to her stomach. She was unsure as to whether or not to get up or stay in bed. She decided on the latter. The decision, though, was not as good an idea as she originally thought as she tried her best to race to the bathroom in time. When the waves finally passed, she sat on the edge of the tub. *My God*, she thought, trying to wash her face with cold water. *It has been a long time since I have had the flu, I can't even remember the last time I threw up like that.*

Trying to stand up and go to the medicine cabinet to get something for her stomach, she found she had no balance, no strength to her legs at all. She would wait for a few moments, think the dizzying feeling had passed, and try to stand again, only to have to sit once again.

"Jessica!" she yelled out, then waited to hear a response from her daughter. "Jessica!" she yelled louder. This time she heard the sound of her child's footsteps coming down the stairs with the patter right behind her of lighter footsteps. Both girls came running in the bathroom.

"What's wrong, Mommy?" Jessica asked, concerned.

"Honey, I think Mommy's got the flu, can you help me get to the bed?"

Jessica did her best to help guide her mother to the bed. Casey ran beside her, holding to her hip as if she was helping her mother as well. Deedra climbed back in, and the girls sat on the sides of it with her.

"What can I do, Mom?" Jessica queried.

"Nothing, honey, thank you for your help. I'm going to call Aunt Marcy and see if she can bring me some Ginger Ale, that should take care of the problem. Will you do me a favor and be good girls and watch TV quietly?"

"Sure we will," Jessica and Casey answered simultaneously.

Deedra was cat napping when her friend arrived, accidentally waking her when she walked next to the bed.

"How long have you been here?" Deedra questioned.

"Not long, I got your Ginger Ale. Here, take a sip." Marcy checked her head for a fever and found none. "You sure it's the flu?" Marcy inquired.

"I don't know what it is, but I'm sick to my stomach and my legs are really weak and unsteady. It woke me up, whatever it is, now I can't seem to get enough sleep."

"Well, how 'bout we call the doctor and go in and make sure that's what you have," Marcy stated

"I don't know about all that, Marcy, for the flu?"

No quicker did the words come out of her mouth than she felt as if she was going to throw up again. Marcy helped her to the bathroom. The Ginger Ale she had just sipped was coming up violently.

"Maybe I should go," Deedra managed to say after the last episode, holding her head up from the toilet.

"OK, let me go call Mrs. Baker, then I will call your doctor. Think you're done? I'll put you back in bed."

Gawd, why do they never have decent magazines to read! Marcy complained to herself, waiting on Deedra to come out of the doctor's office. *What is taking so long anyway?* She checked her watch and realized they had been there for close to an hour.

At last, the door opened and Deedra walked through with the help of a nurse. Her face was extremely pale. Marcy jumped up and walked over to her, taking over the position from the nurse. She didn't realize just how sick she was until she saw her face.

"Well, did the doc give you something to take?"

"Nope!" Deedra answered rather sharply.

"Why not, what did he say?" Marcy inquired. "Is it some kind of flu?"

"Oh no, no Flu! Couldn't be as simple as the flu," Deedra answered, the tone of her voice extremely upset. She sat down in the nearest chair. "Oh no!" she repeated, looking up at Marcy. "Couldn't be as easy as the flu."

"Well then what the hell is it?" Marcy demanded impatiently, tired of playing the "what is it" game.

"They call it Preg-nan-cy, Marcy!" Deedra said, extending the pronunciation of the words, being spiteful.

"Oh my God! What? Oh my God! That never dawned on me, I mean, I never thought about that."

"Well damn, neither did I, thank you." She was being ill-tempered. "Neither did I," she said again in a more somber voice.

For most of the ride home, Marcy asked question after question, nervously trying to have a conversation with Deedra. But Deedra wanted no part of the rapid-fire rhetoric coming from Marcy. Deedra was in shock; never had it dawned on her that she might be pregnant. Even though thinking about it now, it really should have. *We didn't use any kind of protection. Hell, for that matter I haven't been on birth control since Craig died. Good Lord, how stupid can I be.*

The doctor had explained to Deedra that she was having a bad case of morning sickness, that she was dehydrated and needed to increase her fluid intake. Because of that, he wanted her to be in bed for a day or so with plenty of fluid intake until her strength was regained.

Overall, though, she was in perfect shape for this baby if she took good care of herself. She was six weeks along. *Pregnancy!* That is all that kept rattling around in Deedra's head.

The other thought was why now. What was Josh going to say? Oh, she knew what he would want marriage immediately! She just did not think that being pregnant should push them into something she still was not ready for. This was the worst time for this to happen.

"When are you going to tell Josh?" Marcy asked, breaking the silence.

"Not right now, Marcy, I think this needs to wait till after Christmas," she responded.

"*Christmas?*" Marcy's voice was raised. "Are you crazy? Why wait till then?"

"Because I don't want the holidays disrupted! That's why."

"I think Josh would love this for a present, Deedra." Marcy looked over toward her friend, waiting for the answer.

"The time isn't right, not yet."

Marcy didn't press it any more than that; this was something that Deedra would have to work out for herself. Eventually, she would have to tell Josh what was going on, it was not as if she could hide this from him for very long, and he would begin to notice the changes to her body.

"Marcy? I'm sorry, honey, I don't mean to be so short with you. You didn't do this."

"Oh, it's OK. I guess I would be the same way if it were me." Marcy reached over and patted her hand.

"All I want right now is to lie down, I will worry about the rest later. OK?"

"Yeah, I understand."

Chapter 19

Josh had a long day ahead. The calves needed tending, and there were pregnancy checks and a fence on the north side that needed mending. He watched the school bus that took Darrin and Dusty to school, waving as it drove away. It was a great feeling to have his sons there every day, getting on and off the bus. He delighted in being able to show them hands on what they needed to know about the ranch. He wanted them to appreciate it as much as he did. After all, it wouldn't be that many years down the road that both Deacons' children and his would decide on who would take care of the ranch.

By then, he would be the old man watching from afar, as his dad had done with his sons. Too many ranches and farms were going up for sale in this part of their world; subdivisions with houses on top of houses were taking over the once beautiful land around them. Each house in the Deed-Restricted subdivision sat on only an acre of land.

He hoped that the same fate would not befall the McKenzie Ranch. If just one of the kids would take up an interest and love it as much as Deacon and he did, then the tradition would carry on.

His mind stopped speculating when he saw Stubbs come bouncing by him, and he chuckled aloud at that big old furry animal. *Damned ole cat.* He laughed. *He's always into something.* He remembered when he first saw the cat, then a small kitten. A Bobcat kitten is what he was, already bigger than most dogs. Though Stubbs thought he was so much better than the other barn cats around the ranch. He would lounge around on the furniture, taking up the space of entire chairs with his bulky self. Josh would laugh watching the big lumbering animal try to pounce and play with the other much tinier kittens. Josh loved that big ball of fur. He was Josh's companion during the lonely times of his life, especially during the days when he would beg and plead with Lindsey to let him see his boys. The nights were long and suffering, as he wondered if she was treating them all right, wondered if they thought of him or missed him as much as he did them.

His attention turned to thoughts of Deedra. She would fit in so nicely here if he could ever get her to see that. The image of them working side by side together, he could virtually see her playing and loving the animals. In his eyes, she was like a 60's-style hippy, full of love and life. She looked like a gypsy with her long curly hair flowing freely and little run-around dresses blowing in the breeze, plus a pair of slip-on boots to flit around the barn in.

Her life had been altered to become the wife of a wealthy man, but she was never given the opportunity to form her own identity, to find her likes and dislikes. She was a wildflower, pure and simple, a country woman hidden under designer attire. One with a brilliant mind for business, a fabulous mothering instinct, and a peace-filled personality. He believed her identity was as he thought—simple, pure, gypsy-like. But, whatever she was, she truly was his "Sunshine." No matter what he had to accomplish during the day, she was always present in his mind. He could never seem to get enough of her.

Throughout the last several months, Deedra had opened up like a wildflower sexually. A woman willing to learn anything had replaced the shy and distant woman that she had been when he first met her. She reveled in her own sexuality and was passionate and giving. Though there were a few things she had yet to learn, he knew in time she would, making her his perfect match.

With Christmas nearing, he decided that whether she liked it or not, he would propose marriage to her one more time. He also had it planned to bestow her with the most beautiful ring she could ever imagine. He would find it, and it would be as sparkling and unique as she certainly was in his eyes.

Christmas would also be the first time in many years that he would have his sons with him for the entire season. They wouldn't be shuttled back and forth. They would be at home—their home—and they would be a family throughout the whole Christmas season and be able to ring in the New Year together. Josh couldn't wait to see the light in their eyes when they opened up their presents. He would make this a Christmas to remember for them all.

Until then, it was back to thoughts of work and of what needed to be done and who would be sent to take care of it. McKenzie Ranch had ten full-time ranch hands, two of which were foremen, and another two men that acted as security for the ranch in case of poachers. The ranch housed each of the men and their families in their own private homes built along the front of the vast property. The McKenzies took pride in the fact that of all the ranches in the area, theirs treated the workers with respect and appreciation. Each man was given clean and well-taken-care-of housing. The elder McKenzie had the belief that if a man was happy in his home, paid well and treated with dignity; he would never stray from his job. It must have been true, as several of the men, including the foremans, were fifteen-plus-year workers. The ranch ran like a finely tuned machine. Every man knew his place and felt a part of the family.

Josh told the crew before work that he would be leaving early that day. He had something that must be taken care of before the boys got home from school. He asked Lucy, Deacon's wife, if he was running a little late if the boys could stay with her until he returned. Of course she said she would be glad to.

Later that night, with the small gift tucked in his pocket, he looked over at the calendar. It was November 29th. He could hardly wait. Sitting down on the couch across from the boys he pulled the small blue velvet box from the shirts pocket to look at it just one more time. Popping open the small box, he smiled widely, gazing at the contents. Perfection of beauty. It had taken traveling to six different jewelry stores to find the perfect one, but it had been well worth it.

"What's that, Dad?" Dusty asked inquisitively. Darrin looked up from his Play Station game to see what the fuss was about.

"A surprise for Ms. Deedra," Josh answered.

"Oh, cool! Let me see it," Darrin remarked, walking quickly over to his father.

"Naw, you'll just have to wait," Josh joked.

"Come on, Dad, show us!" Dusty whined.

"Well, if you insist," he said, popping open the small velvet box and showing the intricate wedding rings to the two boys.

"Wow! You're going to ask Ms. Deedra to marry you?" Dusty wondered.

"Well, I'm going to try, son, I'm hoping she will say yes!"

"Oh man, me too. I hope so too. It would be so cool having her for a mom," Darrin chimed in.

Josh smiled at the boys for a moment, thankful they liked Deedra. "You think she'd make a good step-mom, huh?" Josh asked.

"Yeah, I do. She's really nice to us, shoot, I even like her kids," Dusty exclaimed.

"Do we have to call her 'Step-mom' if you get married?" Darrin asked, wondering about his father's use of the word.

"No, not necessarily. What would you want to call her?"

"Well, um, why not 'Mom'?" Darrin questioned.

"You have a mom, are you sure that's what the two of you want to do?"

"Yeah, I do. I mean, yeah we have a mom, I guess. But, Ms. Deedra, well—she treats us kind of special," Dusty responded.

Later that evening, in the quiet of his bedroom, Josh opened the small box again, admiring his purchase. It was the perfect ring. The ring was composed of two 14 kt gold hearts, and inside each of the hearts was a beautiful quarter carat ruby with tiny glowing diamonds in the shape of the heart surrounding each of the rubies. Josh fingered the second ring in the box, its perfect mate. It was a band of tiny rubies set in the same 14 kt gold.

Not a bad choice for an ole country boy. Josh beamed, laying the engagement ring back into the box with its match and closing the lid.

Looking down, Stubbs was sitting at his feet purring in the growl-like purr he had. Josh bent down and pulled at his tail a little, thinking that maybe Stubbs would want to fight at his hand, play a little. Instead he just looked at him for a moment and laid back down on his side. "You're so damn lazy, you silly cat," Josh remarked and pulled at Stubbs tail again to see if he could get a reaction. Stubbs just looked at him as if to say, "Would you leave me alone?" So Josh gave up trying to get the big ole cat and readied himself for bed.

Chapter 20

Deedra woke to the nausea that had seemed to have taken control of her throughout most of the night. This was the fourth time she had dealt with this, just making it to the bathroom in time. Once the wave had passed, she went back, sat down on the edge of the bed, and sipped the Ginger Ale she had in the glass next to the bed.

Good Lord, she thought to herself. *This child is going to be a hateful little thing.* She had never been sick to her stomach with either of the girls. Deedra pulled a notebook and pen out from the nightstand drawer, deciding that she would calculate exactly when she thought the baby would come. After adding the six weeks into the mix and rounding it all down with the last period, she figured the baby would come into the world sometime at the end of July, maybe the first week of August.

She must have gone back to sleep, because she was startled awake by a noise. She listened carefully to see if she could hear the sound again. It was someone knocking at the front door. *Oh, the door. That is just great, and I look like crap.*

Just as she reached the door she could see out of the small peephole who it was even before asking. It stopped her cold in her tracks for a moment; she looked like something the cat had dragged in.

"You gonna make me wait out here all day? Open the door, will you?"

"Wait a minute, Josh, at least let me comb my hair!"

"I didn't come to see your hair, woman, now let me in." He chuckled.

131

No sooner did Josh make eye contact with Deedra than he realized she was very sick. She was so pale with big circles under her eyes, and yes, her hair was a complete disaster.

"My Gawd, baby, what is wrong with you?"

"I have some sort of bug, the doctor said," she lied.

"Why didn't you call me? I could have come in and cared for you! I havn't heard a word out of you in two days!" His voice a bit on edge from worry.

"It's just the flu, Josh, I didn't want to bother you with it."

"Bother me with it? Damn, I thought you were busy finalizing the restaurant deal or something and that's the reason you hadn't called. I hate imposing on you when you're busy like that. I tried calling you last night and didn't get any answer, so I decided I would drive in tonight."

"Like I said, it's just this stupid flu."

"Well, where are the girls?" he questioned, realizing they had not come running to jump up in his arms as they usually did.

"Marcy took them home with her a couple nights ago so I could rest."

"A couple of nights ago? Well, OK then—just get back in bed! You want me to fix you some soup or somethin'?"

"No, I'll be fine, go on home and stop worrying," she told him, trying to get him to leave, afraid the charade would be up.

"You've got to be kidding me. I'm stayin' right here, Sunshine."

Great! Deedra thought. *That's just great.*

Josh followed her back into the bedroom. *Why can't he just go home?* Deedra wondered, watching Josh fix the bed before she laid down again.

"I'll tell you one thing, hon, even when you're sick your eyes still sparkle."

An alarm went off in her mind when he said that. She remembered what they said about pregnant women and the "glow thing" that they are supposed to have.

"Awe, that's sweet, Josh," she muttered, not knowing what to say.

"Well, I love you, baby, don't do this to me anymore. When you're sick, you call me!"

"I promise I will, Josh, I just didn't want to bother you with it. Go on home, I promise you I will be fine."

Deedra positioned herself up on her pillows for better comfort and in doing so was looking straight across the room to her dresser. Her legs started to shake and her stomach did a flip when she saw the small white pamphlet on the dresser. Marcy had been looking at it last night and must have laid it over there. It was the standard pamphlet the doctor gave her that told about the prenatal vitamins he had given her to start taking.

Oh my God! She jolted, the pang of fright rising up in her throat. She wondered how to distract him long enough to get over to the dresser and put that in a drawer so he wouldn't see it. Why on earth was he here anyway, for crying out loud, didn't he have work at the ranch to do? Why did he have to show up unannounced?

"Hey, Josh?" She swallowed hard. "Would you mind going and getting me some more Ginger Ale?"

"Of course I can, baby. Anything else you want? Maybe some toast?"

Ugh, toast, she thought to herself and then a light went off in her head. *Yeah, toast! That would give me time.*

"Maybe I should, Josh, if you don't mind."

"You got it, I'll be right back."

Deedra watched as he got up from where he was sitting on the edge of her bed next. All he needed to do was turn and go out of the room and she could have the pamphlet hidden before he had time to return. Instead of turning right away from the bed, he turned to the left. He stopped in front of the dresser and took a look at himself in the mirror right above it. It was a terrible habit he had. If there was a mirror, he had to see if his hair was combed.

With her eyes burning a hole in his back, afraid of what might happen if she looked away, she watched his every move. She prayed in silence that he wouldn't look down. She was angry with him for not just getting up and going out of the room as she expected him to. For that matter, once again, why hadn't he just stayed in the country?

She stared at his eyes in the mirror as he looked at himself; she observed his eyes as they fell to the top of the dresser. Her heart quickened. Her mouth went dry instantly. Her hands started to tremble. She watched in horror as he picked up the small white book, read the exterior of it and opened it to reveal the contents. She saw the change in his facial expressions, his jaw becoming rigid the more he read. His teeth clenched together. Turning back toward the bed, he walked over to where she was lying. Not a word had been spoken. His face was filled with anger. His eyes stared into hers. He threw the pamphlet at her, and it landed in her lap.

"So, you have the flu! A bug, isn't that what you said?" he stated harshly.

Deedra tried looking in his eyes. He turned his face from her. She was so sorry that he had found out this way; she wished that she had been given more time before she had to tell him.

"So how far along are you? Or let me guess, I don't have a right to know that either, right?"

"I'm six weeks along," she whispered.

"When were you going to tell me? When it was born?" he yelled, the anger still so evident in his eyes. There was a seething burning red where the whites of his eyes should have been.

"Don't you yell at me, I just found out!" she shouted back.

"Oh, really? So then you haven't had this flu for a few days?"

"Yes, but—I didn't know. I didn't know I was pregnant until I got sick."

"That's still time I didn't know, Deedra, I mean I know I'm a dumb old redneck and all, but doesn't the mother usually tell the father the same day she finds out?" His voice was still elevated.

"Calm your voice down, Josh! I was going to tell you," she barked back.

"When? When were you going to tell me?"

"I wanted to wait till after Christmas—"

"After Christmas?" He cut her words off. "You weren't going to tell me till after Christmas?" Now the anger and hurt was so prevalent, he had tears streaming down his face.

"It's not like that, Josh, I just didn't want to disrupt everyone…" Her voice was breaking, as she was trying to fight back her own tears.

"Disrupt? You're having my baby! How exactly is that disrupting? I can't believe this, Deedra! I trusted you. Thought you were different. You don't trust me enough to tell me about my own baby? Think it's a disruption?" His voice cracked; the tears overflowed on to his cheeks. Josh tried to wipe them as quickly as they were falling.

Deedra burst into tears, seeing his tears. "You can trust me! I'm not trying to hurt you. I was, I don't know, trying to wait for the right time."

Josh's anger softened, seeing the tears stream from her eyes. Through the tears, she tried to explain that she just wanted to wait and not upset the children's Christmas or their lives with this news. This was new to her; she had never expected to be pregnant again. The shock of the news was something she wanted to get used to before telling him.

But, even with her own tears, Deedra looked into Josh's eyes and understood what his tears were for. Yes, he was angry with her for not telling him about the baby. But, the tears also came from him feeling that once again she was rejecting him in some way by not telling him something that was so important to their lives. This man, a man of stone and hardness, was crying because he felt helpless and betrayed by her.

That is exactly what Lindsey had done to him, left him helpless and betrayed. Now, the woman he loved with all of his heart was doing the same thing by not sharing the most important moment in their lives.

Deedra stood up from the bed and went to him, wrapping her arms around him tightly. His sobs became louder, releasing many years of pain, the pain of loss of a father, of a marriage, of his ex-wife leaving her children, of failed relationships.

Still exhausted, Deedra eased him over to the bed and then climbed on it, motioning Josh to sit next to her. "I'm so sorry, Josh, I wasn't thinking." She scooted over in the bed and patted the bed for him to lie down next to her. He did. It was shocking to see a man cry; never in her life with her father or Craig did she ever see them show emotion.

He was more man than she had ever known. No matter how hard edged, strong and determined in life he was, his emotions flowed profoundly within him. He could be cut to the bone, and he wasn't afraid to show it like most men were. This man, this Josh McKenzie, was a real man in every sense of the word.

"I love you, Josh, I really do. I would never hurt you intentionally. I never thought to look at it from your point of view. I am so sorry about that." She was holding him tightly, kissing his face as she spoke.

"You must think I'm some kind of baby, crying like this." He wondered why in all his life, only since meeting Deedra had this side of his emotions come out.

"No, I don't, I think you're more of a man than most men will ever be!"

He lay there enjoying her touch, her warmth, and her smell.

Deedra really didn't have the energy for it, she still felt so sick, but for the first time in her life, she felt so connected to him that she wanted to touch him, love him. He was sexier now at this moment than he ever had been before.

Quietly she allowed her fingers to touch his face and neck. This was all new to her, to be the aggressor. She had never loved a man in the way she wanted to with Josh. She wasn't even sure she would be able to, or that her illness at this moment would stay at bay long enough to let her try.

She lifted his t-shirt up from around him, bringing it up to his chest, letting her fingers touch the muscles of his stomach and chest. Josh looked at her; the tears were fading now into stains along the sides of his face. He moved his hand to grab for hers.

"What are you doing? You're sick—"

"Shhhhh, just be quiet," she interrupted, whispering.

"But—" He tried to speak again.

"Just let me do this, please," she begged of him.

He didn't argue.

No words were spoken as she started to undress him, removing his shirt from over his head and laying him back down beside her. Josh raised his hips and brought his jeans down from his waist, exposing the fact that once again, he didn't have any underwear on.

Deedra chuckled to herself at that. Did he ever wear them?

After the clothing was removed, Deedra climbed over him in a straddled position and started kissing his face, his neck, and arms. This was uncharted territory to her, with no guideline to go by as to what to do. Nevertheless, she was going to try to figure it out on her own. Moving slowly down his taut body, her tongue kissed the curves of the outline of muscle. Using her tongue the way she had felt Josh use his against her skin, she marveled at the way the tight muscles quivered under the velvety licks.

She stopped for a moment, looking up to find his eyes were closed. The smile on his lips told her he was enjoying this moment. The rock-hard member between his legs told her she was doing a fair job so far. Deedra continued letting her moist tongue slowly slide its way across his body. She felt the hardness between his legs pulsate. She liked this newfound power, the power to dominate and control what he received.

Slowly she moved her body down his, careful not to put any of her weight on him, coming to rest between his legs. She moved her legs to the inside area of his legs and opened them outward so that she could crouch between them.

Beginning with her tongue against the soft tissue of his inner thighs, she then gently began licking the testicle area, feeling them contract under her tongue's swirls. Carefully, she sucked at the skin, then licked each of them slowly, methodically, allowing the tongue to make little circles. She twirled her tongue around the area and then lapped upward. She could tell by his movements and the sounds from his throat that he was enjoying this.

Deedra brought her right hand up to cup around the pulsating hardness. She marveled at the feel of it, the rigid feel to it. This thrilled her beyond anything she had ever imagined. The thrill of the sounds coming from him, coupled with her own sounds of licking, made her just as excited.

He brought his hands down to hold either side of her face. "Are you sure you want to do this?" he asked, his ability to speak muffled.

"Oh yes, Josh, oh yes!"

She put the throbbing hardness in her mouth and moved up and down the shaft with Josh's hands gently holding her head and helping her along. She could tell by the sounds he was making, the way his hips were moving up and down with her mouth, that this pleased him. Josh held her head at a steady, slow, rhythmic pace. He didn't want to get too carried away by the feeling to gag her or be too aggressive and scare her off. But it was driving him insane to have to go so slow when what he really wanted to do was push himself into her mouth hard and fast, releasing all of himself into her.

He dropped his right hand down from her head, taking her left hand into his, he showed her where to hold his engorgement at the base, and by doing so would be able to control the progress herself. This was her first time, he wanted her to feel in control and learn from what she was doing.

When the feeling came over him, he reached for her head to pull her away from him.

"What's wrong?" she questioned.

"Nothing, baby, its time, come up here."

"No, I want to finish this," she cooed.

"You're sure about this?"

"Oh yes!"

Deedra went back to her position, recreating what she had been doing, listening intently for the deep throaty moans to return. Josh brought his hands back down to either side of her head, holding her head steady.

She felt Josh's back arch. She heard the animalistic sounds from deep within his chest. She felt the hot liquid sweetness hit the back of her throat. Choking a bit from the new experience, she tried her best to devour and revel in it, wanting him to be pleased with her for her first experience at pleasing a man. She was pleased with herself for what she was capable of, delighted that she had quenched the fire within.

Chapter 21

That next afternoon, Deedra and Josh gathered the children together at the ranch for the talk. Both of them were apprehensive about telling them and how they would feel, more so on Deedra's part than Josh's. After all, his children already knew, though he hadn't told her that. It took much coaxing to talk her into telling the children as it was. She thought it was much too soon for them to know, but he felt as if they deserved to know everything going on in their lives with no secrets.

Deedra was completely shocked to find that the children took it as just a happy event they couldn't wait to see occur. Everything seemed to be going a lot easier than she could have imagined it would.

The children talked openly with their parents about the future, arguing over whether it would be a boy or a girl. Of course, Darrin and Dusty wanted a boy, and of course the girls did not.

Deedra felt as though some sort of force had taken over her life. She was so afraid she wasn't ready to make this commitment. She was frightened of the future and what it held for her.

This was not the ideal situation. It was certainly not what she had anticipated. It would have been easier if they had the time needed to grow together, not thrust together so quickly because of an impending baby.

She did love Josh; she did want to be with him and did want the new life that was growing inside of her. Yet, she worried about the future and what it would mean to each of them. Especially marriage. Marriage seemed like another lifetime, someone else's life. She could not shake the feeling that something terrible would happen if she gave in to what Josh wanted most, for them to be married. After the children had departed to playing outside, Josh walked over and sat down next to her.

"We really do need to get married, Sunshine," he began. "Say, like Christmas Day?"

"Why so soon, I'm not sure I'm ready for that yet, Josh. It seems way too soon," she answered, sounding worried.

"Look, honey, I know this whole thing scares you. But, with the baby now, I hoped you would change your mind."

"I just don't know, Josh, I'm scared—"

Josh stood up during mid sentence, walked over to the stairs and went up them. She watched him until he was out of sight, sure that he had walked off because he was upset with her. Deedra wished she could just say yes to him and let it go at that. It simply was not as easy as that. She was afraid that she would eventually lose what she and Josh had. They were so close, and in many ways much to close for her comfort.

Her mind wandered to the past again, a place that she had left alone for several months. She remembered her parents' death, how she spiraled into a deep dark depression and low self worth. The marriage to Craig. The sense of protection she thought she had with that marriage. The loss of everything she had known with his death. What if something happened to Josh? There would be no surviving that loss.

The pounding of footsteps coming down the stairs stopped the thoughts for the moment. Her eyes fixed on him walking toward the couch, watched as he sat and turned toward her. He extended his hand open to within inches of Deedra's face, showing the small blue box held within it.

With his other hand he opened the tiny box, looked at her to see her reaction to what was before her eyes. She let out a small gasp when she saw the rings shining up at her.

"Oh, Josh, they're beautiful!"

"Yes they are, Deedra, I searched everywhere for them. Now listen to me, will you?"

She looked into his eyes, nodding.

"I ain't the best guy in the world for you. Hell, I know you could do better with your kind of style and class..." He paused for a moment, taking in a long deep breath, then continued. "Fact is, I love you, I want to share my life with you. I am fully intent on fighting with you!" He stopped briefly, looking to see the reaction so far. "I will argue with you or whatever I have to do with you to get you to marry me!" He broke off, waiting for an answer.

"Josh, I just don't—"

"Deedra, I won't leave this be, I love you too much to let you go now or ever."

He had every intention to bug her with it, repeatedly ask or whatever he had to do to get her to say "Yes." From the moment he saw her until this second, he felt connected to her. She was the woman he wanted to spend the rest of his life with. She was fiery enough to hold him at bay and help keep him in control, yet gentle enough to soften the anger that lay within.

Josh also believed he knew what she wanted as well. Not that he wanted to "own" her or "dominate" her, but she was still like a frightened child in many ways. She never had the chance to stand strong on her own. In order to find the untapped strength, she needed to feel safe in her own skin. If she were challenged, he believed she would be a fierce animal, with the capabilities to endure and withstand any obstacle in her path.

Watching the wheels turning in her pretty little head, he could almost see in her eyes that she was going to say "no," but she just couldn't find the reasons, the really good ones, to tell him.

"Deedra! I mean it, girl, now come on, you have got to marry me, make me a happy man in this life."

Deedra sat there for what seemed like forever, quietly thinking, staring at him. Fear was deeply imbedded in her heart. She was immensely afraid, wanting to say no to him. No, she just couldn't do this. The words wouldn't form in her mouth. If only the phobias she faced would subside long enough for her to make a rational decision. They did have a baby coming, the children were accepting of the marriage, they even expected it, he did love her, and she did love him.

"All right," she muttered faintly. "OK, I'll marry you!"

"All right, now you're talkin!" he screamed out, jumped off the couch, then let out a loud whooping sound. "Wooweeeeeee!"

She was not very thrilled by the idea of this, yet clearly there was not a clear reason to say no. She wished there was more time to sort this out in her mind; everything was happening so fast. Nonetheless, it was going to happen. She was going to marry him, she was having his child. It seemed as though her love for Josh had just begun. What if she was unable to live with someone like him? He was so domineering, and at times very pretentious. *Could she live an eternity with him?* she wondered, having veiled reservations of what tomorrow would bring, coupled with the gnawing intuition that something would go wrong if she felt too comfortable in her life....

Josh was so content with the fact that she said yes that he was totally unaware of her puzzled look. He was so pleased that his dreams were coming true.

Deedra busied herself, jotting down everything that came to mind in her date planner. Christmas was not that far away, there would be a lot of things to deal with before they married. In the morning, she would call Marcy with the news and ask for her help with the wedding. She also wanted to talk to Marcy and Brad about her house. If Marcy and Brad wanted it, it was theirs to have. If they decided it was too much house for them, then she would put it on the market.

Josh gave her full rein to decorate the house any way she liked. Between now and Christmas they would begin to move everything from her house to his.

Marcy was thrilled the next morning when she received the call from Deedra. Marcy understood her friend's reservations regarding the marriage, but knew that with time Deedra would settle right into being Mrs. McKenzie. She was pleased that Deedra, without realizing it yet, would finally get everything her heart would desire out of life.

Of course, she was thrilled at being asked to be the matron of honor as well, but when Deedra told her that she wanted her and her family to have her house, she broke down in tears. Deedra had done so much already by giving them the Fireside; she was stunned and thrilled by yet another wonderful surprise.

Over the next two weeks the two women were together constantly, shopping for the wedding, moving some of Deedra and the children's clothing, having the movers set up to move the large items she was taking, giving Marcy items she wanted and setting up for the women's shelter to come and pick up the remaining furniture.

When they had taken care of the last detail of Deedra's old house, they started to decorate the new. Deedra was becoming more comfortable with each passing day. The children certainly were. They had taken right up in the country, enjoying every waking moment of their new lives.

On more than one occasion, Josh would come in from working outside to see yet another change that had taken place within this domain. He could not believe how beautiful it was becoming, and he couldn't believe that Deedra was decorating everything in a country-americana theme. He knew it was not her style, so he assumed that some of this decorating was for his comfort rather than hers.

The decision was made one evening that they would marry under the huge old oak that sat nearest the pond to the front of the property. Josh had talked with the family's pastor, Reverend Mitchell, and he would perform the ceremony for them. Everything seemed to be running right on schedule, one week prior to the wedding.

The cake, decorations, and food were ordered. The invitations were sent out, all the platforms needed had been built; now it was time for the wait.

Sitting on the front porch step, Deedra and Marcy breathed in a huge sigh. It had been a long day for the two of them, but it had also been the fastest and most productive past few weeks as well. Both women looked at each other almost simultaneously. For a December day it was hot, but typical for Florida weather. Both women were dripping with sweat.

Deedra broke into laughter. Marcy looked up at her as though she might have lost her mind.

"So, clue me in, what's so funny?" she asked, sticking her tongue out at her. "What's the joke?"

"No joke." Deedra giggled. "We just look like drowned rats."

"Well, I feel like one." Marcy started to laugh with her friend. "You do look silly!"

"Excuse me? Look at you!" Marcy poked Deedra in the side.

Without warning, Deedra's facial expression changed to a sad, worried look. Marcy noticed the change immediately.

"Now what's wrong?" she inquired.

"Oh nothing. Just, well, Josh really likes my body, what's he gonna think when I'm huge?"

Oh no, not those hormones, Marcy thought to herself, and then she responded to her friend's question. "For crying out loud, Deedra Marlan, he's going to love you no matter how big you get! You have got to quit worrying about such stuff, that man loves you! You might as well sit back and enjoy it.

"Besides." Marcy started to snicker. "You're going to be as big as a whale, you know, so you better hope he loves all of you." She held her hands way out from her own stomach.

Deedra reached out and smacked her on the arm, the sadness in her eyes gone.

Chapter 22

"What are you doing up already?" Marcy questioned her sleepy-eyed friend as she came into the kitchen.

"I couldn't sleep, kept tossing and turning. What about you?"

"Same reason," Marcy replied, smiling. "Just think, in a few hours you will be Mrs. Joshua McKenzie."

"I know, I know!" Deedra did in fact know—it is what kept her up tossing and turning most of the night. There were a million reasons why she shouldn't go through with this and only one reason why she should: she loved Josh with all of her heart.

The night before last, it felt so perfect sitting in front of the fireplace with Josh and the children, it had felt so right. They were a family sitting there. A family opening up their Christmas presents early.

Now, standing in Marcy's kitchen, she was not quite as sure.

"Where's he taking you for your honeymoon?" Marcy quizzed.

"I don't have a clue, Marcy, but I'm sure you do! After all, you will have the children while we're gone."

"Oh, that's right, I do know, don't I?" Marcy giggled coyly.

"Well, then tell me where I'm going."

"Oh I couldn't do that, Deedra. Nope, sorry, I sure can't tell you a thing." Marcy was chuckling, enjoying the very fact that she knew something her friend didn't.

"Marcy?"

"Yes?"

"Did you know you're a brat!"

"I know, ain't I neat?" Marcy laughed out loud.

Between the two women, they had drank nearly three pots of coffee and reminisced about every aspect of their lives, both the good and the bad. The women hugged like they had never hugged before. Both were coming to realize that Deedra's world was going to be a wonderful trip into the future, no matter what happened.

It had taken much talking on Marcy's part to convince Deedra of that, but finally she realized that she was deeply loved and treasured.

Two hours prior to the wedding, with all of the children showered and in their best dressed outfits, they were ready to go. They were positively excited, each for being able to have the parent in their lives they were so desperately missing. Brad was busy taking pictures of the children all done up in their shades of blue and cream. As per tradition, Deedra had not spent the night at the house with Josh. She had been with Marcy at Marcy's house, and Brad had opted to stay at Josh's house to help get the children ready the following day.

Marcy helped Deedra and herself to get ready. The make-up and nails had been done. Marcy helped Deedra to style her hair up on her head in a bun allowing a few curls to fall about in several areas around her head, then added petite, blue-hued roses and small baby's breath in areas around the bun to give her a sweet romantic look. Last on the list of things to do were the dresses.

The ice cream-colored dress, a mixture of lace over satin with tiny pearl button openings at the back, fell softly around Deedra's shoulders. The dress fit Deedra snuggly, hugging her curves in just the right way to make her body even more well defined. Marcy imagined that Josh would shed a tear the moment he saw her in this dress when she walked toward him today. Marcy wore almost the same style in dress, but hers was ice blue and fit more loosely about her frame then Deedra's dress did.

Marcy called ahead to Brad to have Josh out of the way when they got there so that she could sneak Deedra into Josh's room until time for the wedding to begin.

Katy and Deacon's wife, Lucy, had gotten up early that morning to prepare the house and make sure the catered food arrived on time. They also wanted to be sure, from a woman's point of view, that the children looked wonderful. However, Brad had done a wonderful job of readying the children; the women were a bit surprised and had a laugh between them.

Katy was coming down the stairs when she noticed her son standing next to the foot of the stairs. He had been deep in thought. Up since the crack of dawn, he already had been for a long walk along the fence lines nearest the house and reflected on his life. So many transformations had happened since his marriage to Lindsey. In just a few short hours he would take Deedra as his bride.

Probably the smartest decision I ever made, he had contemplated. *What made her so much different?* He didn't know. He had used so many women after the split with his ex-wife, and had tried diligently to start real relationships after that, but nothing ever meant as much to him as the woman he was marrying today. Perhaps it was because she was so hard to get, a struggle, something he had to work for…

"Son?" Katy called out, breaking the chain of thought he had been in.

"Hey there, Momma." He grabbed her up for a much needed hug.

"I was just thinking something, Josh." She realized that her own flesh and blood was twice the size of her.

"What's that?" he asked.

"I'm gonna have two more grandchildren in just a little bit."

"Oh, Momma, you never stop to amaze me sometimes!" He hugged her tightly again, so pleased that she would accept Deedra's children as her family.

"Hey, you better get to the den, she'll be here soon."

"I know, Momma, I love you."

"I love you too, son," she said, her arms still wrapped around his waist. "You know your daddy would be so proud."

"Think so, Momma?"

"Oh yeah, son, he'd love that girl!"

A tear streamed from the outside corners of his eyes that his dad, the man he thought of as his hero, would have approved of his choice.

In the den, Deacon tried to keep things light with his brother; after all, he was a bundle of nerves pacing back and forth in front of the desk. Deacon knew the time wasn't right for any of his razing remarks he so liked to do with Josh.

Deacon walked over to where Josh was pacing and grabbed him up into a bear hug, surprising Josh that he was displaying any kind of affection. Never had he done that in their whole lives together.

"I know I'm a lousy brother at times, man, but you're doin' the right thing here, so quit pacing."

If the hug surprised him, then Josh was in shock now. He had walked all his life in the shadow of Deacon McKenzie, wishing he could have had a life like his, wishing things in his life had come as easy and always feeling as if he never measured up. Yet, in one hug and few words, Josh finally felt as though he was truly a part of Deacon's life, his brother.

"OK, girls, it's time," Brad called to them behind the closed door.

Marcy turned to Deedra and hugged her. "You ready?"

"I guess," she said nervously. "Wish these butterflies would go away though."

"It will be OK, Deedra. Just look straight at Josh as you walk toward him and you'll be fine." They could hear the music start in the distance.

The guests were sitting in their chairs positioned in a half moon shape around the outer circle of the big oak tree, and a long aisle of light blue carpet divided the chairs. Reverend Mitchell retrieved Josh and Deacon from the den, the three men entering the area together. Katy had made a motion for Brad to get the Matron of Honor to begin her walk. Katy then took her seat next to both Josh and Deedra's children sitting in the white folding chairs on the front row.

She couldn't help but notice there were absolutely no family members on Deedra's side of the aisle, except for about fifteen people, and she assumed they were co-workers. The only "family" sitting in the front row seats were Brad and Marcy's children. Josh had told her that Deedra's parents were both deceased. Didn't she have other family members, a sister, brother—something?

Very odd, she observed, but she didn't have any time to think further into the thought, as the music was beginning to play.

The day was beautifully crisp and clear. Huge fluffy white clouds scattered throughout the bright blue-gray sky. Though it was Christmas Day, it was as warm as if it were summertime. The birds were singing sweet melodic sounds as if they were a part of the musical background.

Katy looked up at her sons standing with their best grey tuxedos on and smiled to herself at how handsome they both were. She looked Josh up and down; he was so handsome with his deep dark skin, his dark mane of hair flowing around his shoulders, shining brightly from the sun's rays.

"Oh that boy." She shook her head to herself. "That long hair, wish he'd cut it."

Josh's eyes met with his Mother's for a second; he gave her a wink and they both smiled at each other. Seeing him up there, nervous and proud, reminded her of a time long since gone.

She was such a young bride, filled with love and hope for the future. She was so in awe of the man that she was to marry, walking down the aisle to meet her beloved Buck McKenzie. She was just sixteen years old, young by today's standards, and Buck had been twenty-four. Nevertheless, from the moment she saw him at the church social she had fallen head over heels for the handsome rodeo star/ranch owner.

He had been on his own working the ranch from the time he was fourteen, and in addition, he had saved just about every dollar he made doing the rodeo circuit as a sideline. Like Josh, he was aggressive and arrogant, and walked right up to her in a crowd of people to tell her she was "the most beautiful girl in the whole county" and that he wanted to take her out. Her father had forbid them dating alone, so her younger sister Louise went everywhere she and Buck went. In spite of this, when Buck asked her father for

Katy's hand in marriage, he gave his blessings and the two were wed.

Josh looked so much like his father; he had the same smile and aggressiveness. Her son, their son, had the same dark hair and eyes, the same mischievous smile.

Deacon had more of her family's features—dark, blue-green eyes, yet just as dark skinned as his brother Josh. Both men were handsome to a fault. Especially to a mother's eyes. The memory went on hold for a moment as she caught a glimpse of Marcy coming up the aisle.

The moment Deedra stepped out into the sunlight, Josh had to choke back the tears welling up in his eyes. She was the most breathtaking woman he had ever seen in his life at this moment. He watched her walk toward him, escorted by Brad. All Deedra knew was that her legs were shaking uncontrollably, her hands trembling. Though she hardly noticed once she was able to get a clear glimpse of the handsome Josh.

"Joshua Tyler McKenzie, will you take as your bride Deedra Elizabeth Marlan?" Reverend Mitchell asked.

For a moment, there was not a sound all around them as the crowd waited for Josh to speak. For a moment he could not speak, did not speak; he was in awe of this beautiful woman standing before him. He had watched her walk toward him, the sun to the back of her. He could have sworn there was a golden glow encircling her.

"I will," he finally replied. The tears steadily snuck down the sides of his face.

Deedra had some difficulty as well getting the words out. She had to mentally will herself to choke back on the soft sobs, the shaking of her limbs, and the cracking of her voice in order to answer the questions.

"I now pronounce you husband and wife," Reverend Mitchell rejoiced in shouting out into the crowd. "You may kiss your bride, Joshua!"

Josh reached for Deedra, bringing her close to his body,

wrapping his arms around her; kissing her for the first time as his wife. "My sweet, sweet baby, I will always love you," he whispered, kissing her lips softly.

"I will love you too." She smiled softly.

The reception was a wonderful time of celebration for everyone. Josh and his new bride danced to almost every song played. Deacon had let his guard down and was Two Stepping with Lucy. Brad and Marcy even seemed to be renewing their love for one another. The children were busy playing, dancing, and laughing with each other. Every new Country Music Song played on the large CD player with a Disc Jockey watching over it.

Something about this Christmas day sparked renewed and wondrous desires in everyone's hearts. So, by the time the reception had ended, it seemed that not only were Josh and Deedra whispering passionate secrets in each other's ears, but also other couples, as well as aunts and uncles, seemed to be doing the same.

Josh walked over to his mother and reached his hand out to her. She would get the final dance of the evening before he departed.

Deedra stood on the sidelines and watched as her man—her husband—slowly danced with Katy. It brought a smile to her face to watch. Josh, the man that was always so sure of himself and so cocky, was dancing around the floor with his mother with a look in his eyes as though he owned the world and all that was in it.

So arrogant! She smiled to herself. Nevertheless, that is what she loved about him. Even when he felt insecure, he never let it show to the outside world. He acted as though nothing ever bothered him, he could conquer anything in his path. *The Beast of all Beasts! And so sexy looking!*"

"What you thinking about?" Marcy interrupted.

"Oh, just how wonderful the day turned out," she replied.

"It was beautiful. Look at you!" she said, grabbing for her arm and half spinning her around. "You're absolutely beautiful!"

When Josh returned to Deedra's side, he announced that he was taking his woman and they were leaving. Marcy rushed over to get her goodbye hugs, as did Brad and the children.

Deacon surprised everyone when he walked over and took Deedra's right hand and kissed it gently. "Welcome to the family, Mrs. McKenzie." Then he dropped her hand and made a tipping motion with his hat. He turned and hugged Josh with all the strength he had in him. It was yet another bolt from the blue for Josh. *Two hugs in one day, is the world ending or is Deacon just getting old?*

"The fun will now begin!" Josh announced loudly, as if he were the ringleader at a carnival.

A roar of whoops and hollers could be heard as Josh opened the door and helped Deedra up into his truck.

Chapter 23

The drive seemed endless because Deedra had no idea where she was going. Deedra checked her watch periodically during the long ride. It was around two when they left the reception. It was six-thirty now. She tried refraining herself from asking Josh too many questions about where they were going; he really wanted this to be a huge surprise for her. Finally, though, when they stopped for dinner outside of the Valdosta Georgia exit around seven, she could not wait any longer. Her curiosity had gotten the better of her.

"How much farther?" she asked, fingering her menu and hoping that he would say that it was not much farther.

"You just relax, we have a little bit yet."

"Relax? I can't relax; it's driving me crazy not knowing."

"OK, well, don't know what to tell you then." He snickered.

"You are no fun, Mr. McKenzie; can't you at least give me a little hint as to where we're going? Please?" she begged in a little girl's voice, her lips pouty.

"Nope, no can do. I'm not telling you anything," he grinned. "Now, what are you hungry for?"

"Um, answers?" She winked.

"Um, nope," he mocked.

Several times throughout the meal, she tried her best to get him to leak even the slightest of information. He wouldn't budge. Not one hint. He just sat there with a sheepish grin on his face and shook his head. Both had ordered the steak and baked potato dinner, Deedra moving her food around her plate, too nervous to be hungry. Josh, on the other hand, was devouring his.

By the time they got back to the truck, Deedra thought she would try for one last-ditched effort at finding out a piece of information. Instead, what she got was a firmly planted kiss to her lips. A large grin passed across Josh's face as he patted her butt and watched Deedra jump up in the truck.

With the sounds of the tires humming against the roadway off I-75, Deedra grew sleepy. Leaning over toward the passenger door, she locked it and curled herself up as best she could in her dress. If she had known it would have been this long she would have changed before they left, found something a bit more appropriate for traveling. But Josh had told her not to worry about changing. So here she was in a dress, a nice dress at that, in a truck and trying her best to be comfortable.

As she drifted in and out of sleep, half-listening to the music on the radio, Josh drove the endless roads. To where, she had no idea. The truck motor turning off woke Deedra out of her light sleep.

"We're here finally?" She looked up through the glass of the windshield and saw only darkness. "Where are we?"

"A rest stop. Come on, get out and stretch your legs."

Deedra looked all around her; it was pitch black, all but the light that led the way to the bathrooms. It was a rest stop all right, with no one in sight—it was desolate and much too quiet. She wasn't so sure she liked this at all. She squinted her eyes to see her watch; it was just after eleven. She still had no idea what town she was in.

"Come on, Sunshine." Josh's tone sounded like it was almost ordering her. He reached out for her hand to help her out of the truck. She thought maybe he didn't want her to go the restrooms alone, so she did as he instructed and took hold of his hand. When they walked past the building that held the bathrooms, though, she wondered what he was doing and looked at him inquisitively.

"Where are we going?" she questioned.

"I'll show you, come on," he said, pulling her along by her hand. Stopping in front of a large wooden picnic table, Josh turned toward her, reached down to her hips, and picked her up in one quick swoop, planting her firmly on the edge of the table.

"Josh, what are you doing?" she asked again, a worried look in her eyes. "What's going on here?"

"You ask a lot of questions, don't you?" He smirked. "I decided I couldn't wait any longer," he said, his voice suddenly sounding low and gruff. Unbuckling his belt, he unzippded his pants in a hurried motion, letting them fall to his knees.

"Are you crazy, Josh? Oh my God, what are you doing? Somebody will see."

Josh cut her words off with a fiery kiss and started lifting the lacy dress from around her legs, bringing it up to her hips. He reached for the top of her pantyhose, found the elastic, then motioning for her to lift her hips, he removed both pantyhose and panties down and off in one hurried movement.

"Josh, stop this!" she ordered.

Her words were ignored. He moved her to the edge of the table, pushing her lightly on her shoulders so that she would lie back onto the table's top, and then swiftly scooted her to the edge of the table.

As soon as he positioned himself between her thighs, all the reserve she was feeling left her mind. She closed her eyes and let him take command of her body, hoping no one would come upon him or her in the darkness.

Skillfully he moved his tongue up and down and encircled around the sweet area. He was not going to spend a great deal of time there, just enough to make her wet and receptive to him. He was flickering, lightly licking, then using his tongue to expand the area, starting the motion over again until he felt her hips come up off the table from the feelings deep within her spine. He brought his mouth up to hers and kissed her, making her taste the hot sweetness that was hers.

As soon as he entered her, she exploded again. The thrust became more powerful; it was almost animalistic in the way he was taking her. The thrusts were harder against her than she thought was ever conceivable. When the time came for him to release himself within her, she could have sworn she heard the low growl of a lion.

With her pantyhose and panties ruined from the ground below, Deedra sat up, trying to fix her dress. The night air was chilly against her skin, causing her to shiver once her body temperature returned to normal. Josh walked her back to the bathrooms so that she could rearrange herself and fix her hair. Once back at the truck, he pulled a blanket from behind the seat.

"Take your dress off and put this on."

"You're kidding me, right? Ride naked?"

"Nobody's gonna see you but me," he countered.

"You're nuts, Josh, you're really nuts!" She giggled, a flush of red gold across her face.

"Yep, that I am! But, you like it, don't you?" he commented, winking at her.

As soon as he started the truck up, he informed her they only had about an hour left of travel. Deedra had to admit to herself that wearing the blanket without any clothing underneath made her feel kind of sexy, sinful. Every few miles or so, Deedra would feel daring and would open the blanket and flash herself to him. Josh would try to grab for her, only to have her move away and giggle.

She loved this new game she had of teasing him, learning something new about the woman hidden within. She even liked the thought of what they did at the rest stop. It was wicked, naughty. The thought of being Josh's personal plaything, it made her express a devilish amusement to herself. Anything he would want, she would find a way to give.

Taking one of the exits off the main highway they had been on, she could see that this was a smaller two-lane road. The last sign she had seen said Perry, Georgia. Wherever they were going, it was going to be in the country, she had guessed that much.

The truck then turned off the two-lane road and started down a hard, dirt, one-lane pathway. Now this was a desolate area, much farther into the country than she imagined she had ever been. They were not passing any houses along the way; at least she could not see any house lights anywhere; she strained her eyes to see out into the blackness.

The road turned rough, the truck bouncing their bodies up and down on its black leather seats. The headlights reflecting down on to the small path had Deedra's mind racing as to where they were going. A tent? she wondered. *He wouldn't let me pack any of my things; he is going to keep me in a tent! Ewwwww, I'm going to be sleeping with bugs in a tent. Oh Gawd, I hate bugs.*

Deedra squinted her eyes, trying to make out the small glimmer of lights in the distance. Once the truck lights paved the way closer to the object, she could see that it was a small log cabin. *Phew!* She was instantly relieved that it wasn't a tent after all.

With relief in her eyes, she stepped down out of the truck with Josh's help, to see the front view of the dimly lit porch of the cabin. The cabin was built with some sort of light brown logs, she could not make out the type, but they were vacant of the outer layer. Stepping up onto the porch, she could see that the flooring was made of the same type of wood. There were two light-colored wooden rockers sitting to the left of the front door, and she guessed them to be very old by the style of them.

Josh instructed her to stand there at the threshold of the door and wait for him while he retrieved their gear from the truck.

Returning, he unlocked the door and started carrying the items inside. Deedra picked up one of the large duffel bags to help him but was told that she had to stand right were she was, he would take care of unloading and bringing everything in.

So, she stood there on the porch and watched him go in and out of the entryway repeatedly; Josh didn't speak a word to her with each trip he made.

At last, he came back from inside of the domain that she had yet to lay her eyes on and stood there in front of her.

"Well, you ready to go?" he questioned.

"I've been ready," she replied.

He scooped her up in his arms, carried her over the threshold of the door, and stood her back on her feet just inside.

"OK, here's the deal. You're not to do anything on this trip, Deedra," Josh remarked, holding her close to him. "No questions either, OK?" He cocked his head to one side, waiting for her response. Deedra just looked at him rather oddly, as if she did not understand what he was saying. "You'll see what I mean."

"Um, OK," she answered like a child that had been scorned.

Josh busied himself putting away everything he had brought and then collected the wood for the fireplace. Deedra walked through the bottom floor of the cabin, getting to know her surroundings and marveling at the rustic yet well-kept furniture and handstitched quilts, curtains and wall art.

It had all of the comforts of home: television, stereo, refrigerator, bathroom, and various styles of antique furniture. Each room was small, but so unique and beautifully arranged. She walked upstairs and saw that the entire floor, a loft area overlooking the living room, was as wonderful as the downstairs.

The huge bed was also made of the same type of logs as the house and dominated the room to the extent that only one small dresser and a small white wicker chair had room to fit. Deedra was stunned by the artwork of the quilt that covered the bed and window in this room, realizing that either Josh's mother or grandmother must have made all the items, or they had come from other family members. Perhaps they were gifts when they had married all those years ago.

"Deedra!" Josh yelled from the downstairs living room.

"Yeah, be right there," she said, making herself seen by walking close to the balcony of the loft and then down the staircase.

"I've got the wood for the fire, and I'm ready to light it. I wanted you here when I lit our first fire," he stated, looking up at her.

Aw, now that is romantic, she thought, stepping from the bottom stair to the living room floor.

The birds chirping outside woke Deedra from her peaceful sleep. She immediately rolled over to where Josh had been sleeping the night before. He was gone. Letting her body stretch, she lay there listening closely to see where he might be. Deedra could not hear him, but the familiar aromas of coffee and bacon filled the air, making her ravenous as soon as the smell entered her nose.

Slowly, she rose from the bed like a cat stretching his legs. That was the most comfortable big mattress she had ever been on in her life. A heavily stuffed feather downed mattress was like sleeping on a cloud filled with air.

They had not christened the bed yet. Both were so tired from the events of the day before that they had silently decided to wait to make their first time as a married couple something to remember rather than just a quickie to end the night with. Besides, they had already had the "quickie" when they stopped at the rest stop.

"I smell something wonderful," she sang out, entering the kitchen. There was a wide smile on her face as she saw her new husband preparing breakfast.

"Oh no you don't! Go! Go on, get back in bed!" he demanded. "Don't ruin this, go on."

She wanted to stay, but realized she had walked in on a special surprise he was trying to plan. So without protest, she turned and went back to the bedroom and climbed back into the big comfy bed.

In about ten minutes, she heard the hard steps of Josh coming up the stairs. He had a tray full of goodies for his new bride. He set the tray down across her lap and she looked at all that was sitting on the tray. There were pancakes, bacon, eggs, and two large coffee cups filled with wonderfully dark rich coffee. Sitting on the very end was a small vase with two Gardenias sitting in it, adding a sweet fragrant smell.

Deedra delighted in eating all that he prepared.

"OK, here are the rules for the next two weeks," Josh began, sounding insistent. She started devouring the food and listened intently to him. "You don't lift a finger! When you get back home, you will have plenty to do with bringing this baby into the world. So, this is your vacation!" he said, patting her tummy.

She did not know quite what to say to him; she was in awe of this man. He was so hard to figure out. One day he was as rough a man as could ever be possible, and yet little things he did now and then spoke volumes of his tenderness and thoughtfulness.

"You can go on walks or whatever you want."

"That's sweet, Josh, but this is your honeymoon too," she replied.

"But, we'll do this my way, just this once," he ordered back. "You don't go outside of the grounds of this cabin, though. Not without me!"

"And why not?" she inquired.

"Well, this is a hunting cabin, hon. That means wild hogs and such! If you don't know what you're doing, you can get hurt, understand?"

"Yes, OK," she answered apprehensively. "Are you going to hunt here?"

"Sure am." Josh nodded.

"Can I go with you?" she wondered.

"Don't think you'll like it, but yeah, you can go, I'd love to have you go with me."

"Is this your property?"

"Well, it's ours now, Deedra, My dad left it to me in his will. Sits on two hundred acres of untouched land. Was his since right after he married my momma. Great huntin' grounds here."

Deedra listened as he spoke about the fondest recollections of hunting and fishing with his father on this land, and all the wonderful memories that made this cabin special.

Josh grew quiet for a moment, and Deedra realized he was lost in thoughts of his past. It made her feel sadness for him that they were only memories. Josh looked over into Deedra's eyes when he realized he had stopped talking.

He grabbed for her hand and squeezed them in between his. "One more thing, Sunshine."

"What?" she inquired.

"While we're here I don't want you to wear clothes inside the cabin, and when we're outside, I want you to wear the dresses I bought and hung up in the closet upstairs, OK?"

For a moment, she looked at him, a bit stunned. The odd look returned to her face as she wondered what on earth he meant. Then, she realized that this did not seem so much like a demand, but more like something he wished her to do for him.

"Well, OK, if that's what you want, I guess I can do that. But why?"

"Just trust me on this!"

"All right," she said, still puzzled.

They spent most of the time the first week inside the cabin. Josh loved watching his wife walk around the cabin or sit in front of the fireplace naked. He enjoyed ravishing her body every chance he could, showing her both the tender side to his lovemaking as well as the animalistic side she had learned he possessed early on in their relationship.

At first, Deedra felt extremely self-conscious of her naked body so exposed all the time in front of him. But, by the end of the first week she felt a comfort in it, almost to the point of never wanting to wear clothes again. She was learning to be totally free and uninhibited about herself, like a butterfly coming out of its cocoon. She marveled in the attention Josh gave to her body. She could not, for the life of her, remember what it was that had made her resist Josh for so long. She was glad, though, that he had stuck by and fought the demons within her to finally capture her heart and make her his own.

Josh had his reasons why he didn't want Deedra to wear clothes. First and foremost, he enjoyed watching her body as it moved, the curves and lines of her soft pale skin. He cherished the weight on her hips and tummy, loved that she was not perfect. The small imperfections she had were breathtakingly beautiful to him. It was her body, and the sensuality of that made it perfect to him.

It was a joy laying her down in front of the fire, it being the only light, and touching her growing breasts and stomach. He swore he could tell the difference each time he touched her. This body of hers, being this close to it, would be as close as he would ever be to his unborn child. If he could, he would keep her naked until the very day the baby came so that he would not miss any of the changes taking place.

There was another reason he wanted her naked. He wanted her to feel the freedom of her own body, to realize that she was beautiful and wanted. But, he also wanted her to realize what the power of her own self, what her sexuality, her femaleness, did to him every moment he was with her.

It was not just about the sex, though. Deedra learned that though Josh seemed a bit backwoods because of his southern accent, he was in fact an extremely intelligent man. Many hours were spent in the cabin debating politics, the sciences, religion and the philosophy of life.

The beginning of the second week, Josh woke early and decided to venture out of the cabin to do some hunting. Deedra watched inquisitively as he dressed in his dark camouflaged clothing and tied his long hair back with a thick piece of black leather. Somehow, this made him look different to her. He looked more Indian, more rogue-like than she had seen before.

She studied the transformation he was making into this silent weapon, concealing himself to search out and kill his prey. Watching him, she wondered how he would ever be able to kill an animal when she had seen him build friendships and teach an animal to trust him.

"Can I go with you?" she asked, standing from the bed and walking toward the dresser.

"Get dressed, you can. Realize, though, it's a lot of walking!"

"I want to go; I want to see what you do," she replied.

Deedra grabbed for one of the drab green dresses that Josh had picked out for her to wear when she went outside. They matched the green in Josh's camouflaged clothing perfectly and she had to laugh to herself at that fact. Josh handed her a pair of brown moccasin boots that went almost up to the top of her knees. He watched as she slipped them on and tied the long laces up in the boot. Once she had the boots tied up, he handed her a pair of snake leggings to go on top of them, showing her how to put them on.

God, is this the stupidest stuff to wear. I look absolutely ridiculous! she imagined, fluffing the dress around her knees. *Thank Goodness no one will see me.*

It was not quite six in the morning when they started out the door together. The sun was not yet dawning in the eastern sky. Walking hand in hand, they entered into the thick area of brush that lay beyond the boundaries of the cabin. Josh cautioned her to stay behind him so that he could tramp down some of the brush in their way. This was so far out of Deedra's element, totally out of the realm of things she had ever seen in her life.

Everything he did, he explained to her why he did it that way, teaching her as the day went along. At times, a smile would cross his face; he was thrilled that she was willing to learn. He had never met a woman that wanted to do anything he did. Therefore, this was rare and so very special to his heart.

Deedra walked softly when Josh did. If he crouched down, then she did too. When he stopped to listen, she did the same. She was being taught to watch for the movements and do the same thing he was doing. Deedra marveled at the realization that she was getting quite good at reading his body language and doing what he wanted without having to say a word to her. Without be aware of it, Deedra was learning exactly what Josh wanted her to learn: to be very aware of her surroundings and of him at all times.

They had seen several deer and a few small wild hogs, but Josh had not shot at any of them.

"Hey, I have a question."

"Sure. What?"

"Why didn't you kill that deer back there?"

"Because it was a doe—a female. I don't kill does."

"Why don't you?" she wondered, really having no idea.

"My daddy taught us to never harm the female if you can help it, they carry the offspring for the future, that's why."

"Oh, OK, I understand, I think."

"The female gives us the future, it's simple," he responded.

He was getting a real kick out of teaching her, spending the next hour sitting and explaining to her his way, the way of his dad and what his teachings had meant to him. He was made to understand everything from the time he was old enough to walk the woods with his father without falling down; he always assumed everyone knew what he did.

"Hey, you!" Josh spoke above the whisper he had been speaking to her in. It caught Deedra off guard. "Shuck that dress of yours off and come here! I wanna see what you got."

"Oh, come on now, Josh, not here. You pick some of the oddest times, don't you?" she balked.

"Yes here, and why not?" he urged again, pulling her up to him, his eyes flashing sparkles of gold from the sun.

"But, Josh," she pretended to whine.

"But what? Who's gonna see you out here?"

Moving inches away from him, Deedra pretended to push back away from his grasp. Standing up to remove her dress, it dawned on her that she could have a little fun with him. After all, Josh was right; they were on 200 acres of woods. No one would see anything she did.

Slowly removing her dress, she started teasing him, doing a little strip tease. When the dress was removed, she inched forward, allowing the garment to barely touch his face. Then she began to dance provocatively around him, laughing wickedly.

Josh grinned widely. Not only was she turning him on, but also he could see she was coming in to her own. This new awakening was happening before his eyes. This was what he had been waiting for, the true "gypsy woman" to reveal herself.

When he could no longer stand the wait, he grabbed for her. She sidestepped him and continued her dance. He reached for her again; she let out a marvelous giggle and danced a little closer. This time when he reached out, he caught her arm. He brought her to him and held her tightly.

"You're such a dangerous man, Mister McKenzie," she said, using her best Marilyn Monroe voice.

"Oh you have no idea, baby, how dangerous I can be," he growled back, an evil-looking smile planted firmly to his lips. He was playing with her, and she was aware that he really was no more than putty in her hands. She had the power to control his very existence if she chose to.

Every moment that he could be with her, talk to her, be inside her, he had to be. He ached to see her face, feel her body move beneath him, and feel the passion as it washed over them. She was his obsession.

Chapter 24

There were hugs and kisses all around when Deedra and Josh came home. The children were so excited to begin their new lives with both a mom and a dad that they had been antsy the whole time they were gone.

Marcy and Brad had stayed the last several days at the ranch in order to ready Deedra's girls for the transition to their new home and to prepare them for the new school system they would attend. Jessica and Casey had been busy decorating their new bedrooms with the personal touches they had brought with them from the other house. Josh had told them anything they wanted to do in making their new rooms their own style, they could.

While Josh went off to visit his mother, Deedra had the task of telling everyone the details of the honeymoon. The children were getting a kick out of hearing about the cabin and the wildlife she had seen. While Deedra spoke, a wide smile came over Marcy's face as she watched the pure sunshine radiate from her friend's eyes. Deedra had found the happiness she so desperately needed in her life and it was oozing out every pore of her being.

By nightfall, with the children worn out, Marcy and Brad decided it was time to leave the peacefulness of the ranch and head back to their own home. The kisses of good-byes and goodnights signaled the children to climb the stairs to their beds.

Deedra fell to the couch and lay her head against the back of it. She was extremely exhausted from the long and wonderful two weeks they had, plus the hours spent on the drive home. She was ready to begin a new life that just weeks before had scared her to death.

Josh walked through the living room with the baggage in hand and had to stop in his tracks for a moment and drink in the splendor of his sweet wife asleep on the couch, curled up like a small kitten. Kneeling down in front of her, he planted a soft kiss to her lips, waking her.

"Where are the kids?" he whispered.

"All safely tucked in bed," she answered sleepily.

"Come on and go too, sleepyhead, I'll say goodnight to them and tuck you in while I'm up there."

"Aw, Josh, you are so sweet," she whispered.

"Shhhh, don't tell anyone." He laughed.

When morning came, Deedra rolled over to find Josh was gone, as usual. He had such a habit of waking before her, sleeping only five or six hours a night. Quiet as a mouse he would leave, off to do the daily routine of running the large ranch. *Ah yes, our bed*, she thought, touching the area next to where Josh had been. *Our bed*, she repeated. *Our house...our lives...our children.*

The months flew by faster than she could have imagined. With each passing day, the summer months' sun was getting hotter. Such is the way of life in Florida, with warm winters and extremely hot summers. It was the beginning of June; Deedra's stomach was enormous. It was so much bigger than it had been with her other two children. Her walk, the distinct waddle, was very prominent, and she was already having a hard time with putting on shoes. In spite of this, her doctor, Dr. Rapin, had listened repeatedly to the heartbeat and checked her health constantly. Through his measurements of her abdomen, he believed the baby would be large. Other than that, her pregnancy was coming along quite well.

It worried her, though. Just how "big" would the baby be, especially with her looking as if she should deliver any day now and yet only a little over seven months along.

Sitting at the kitchen table enjoying her morning coffee, she allowed her hands to encircle the hard protruding area, letting the baby kick back at her when she pushed in on her stomach. She loved doing this. It would make her giggle at the small bundle. Little Bumpkin did not like to be crowded any more than his father did. Probably just as ornery and contrary too. She smiled.

Two weeks from now, the appointment was set for the ultrasound. She and Josh would find out then what the sex of their unborn child would be. They were supposed to have it done back when she was five months along, but at the last minute, both had decided they didn't want to know. They would await the birth to find out.

However, from then until now, it had been eating away at them. When they could no longer stand the wait, both decided to go ahead with the ultrasound after all, cursing themselves for not finding out when they had the chance. Consequently, Deedra made the ultrasound appointment. This time they would find out, though it seemed like forever before the scheduled date would arrive.

The sound of someone screaming her name from out near the front porch startled Deedra, taking her away from her deep thoughts. Quickly she stood from the table just as Lucy was racing through the door. Automatically her heart sank to her feet and she felt chilled to the bone. Fright surrounded her mind like a thick fog with the sight of Lucy in some form of distress.

"My God, Lucy! What's happened?" Deedra demanded, frightened by the pale expression on Lucy's face.

"It's Josh, honey! We have to go, he's been hurt," Lucy shouted nervously.

"Oh God, Lucy! Oh God no! Oh no!" Deedra screamed out, hoping beyond hope that it was just a huge mistake.

"Get your purse! Deedra, come on! Where's your shoes?" Lucy was racing through the living room like a mad man, searching for the items without really focusing on what it was she needed to find. Deedra was right behind her, asking questions, her shoes being the least of importance right now.

"What happened? Lucy! Tell me what happened!" she screamed, trying to get her attention. "Where is he?"

Lucy was not answering any of the questions. She was in single-minded mode, searching for the purse and shoes. Her thoughts called to her repeatedly—Get Deedra to Josh as soon as possible.

"Why won't you answer me?" Deedra cried out. "Tell me what happened? Where is he? Lucy!" Deedra's mind was in a panic, the tears flowing even harder. Deedra repeated the question again, finally grabbing at Lucy's arm, turning her in a half spin.

Only then did Lucy realize she hadn't answered her. "He's been hurt—hurt real bad, Deedra. We have to get to the hospital!"

Deedra outran Lucy to her car as soon as she said that. Josh needed her; she no longer cared if her shoes were found or not. She would go just the way she was.

"Tell me what happened, Lucy," Deedra sobbed, trying to calm herself unsuccessfully, the tears flowing like a river down her face.

Lucy sped toward the highway, trying her best to get out the words. "A bull caught him. A bull they had in the cow pens, he went wild on them! I haven't seen him, Deedra, they came and got me. He tried to get out of the way, didn't see it coming."

"Oh good God, Lucy! Did they say how badly he's hurt?"

"He's hurt bad, that's all I know. He tried to roll under the fence and couldn't get out of the way," Lucy exclaimed.

Lucy hated having to be the one in this position, the one that had to tell Deedra. She had never been great at dealing with such confrontations. She was a true basket case when an emergency occurred. But, besides that, this was the last thing Deedra needed at this stage of her pregnancy, to be put under this much stress. But, what else could have been done? Someone had to get her to the hospital, and she had been the one elected to have to tell her.

"Where is he, Lucy? I mean, which hospital?" she demanded.

"Tampa General, took him by helicopter."

"Helicopter? Oh God, oh God!" Now there was no denying it, Deedra knew it was extremely serious; the closest hospital to them was Manatee Memorial. Tampa General was two hours away by vehicle, and was the hospital used for severe trauma or burn victims. "Where did it happen?"

"Out in the back cow pens, they got him help as quickly as they could, Deedra."

This cannot be happening, it just cannot be happening, Deedra thought, letting her body rock back and forth with nervous energy. She wished they could fly to the hospital as well.

Deacon had gone in the helicopter with Josh to the hospital. There was no way the paramedics could have kept him from going. Never in his life had he ever been this frightened of anything, but seeing his brother, seeing what he went through—he was scared to death. His mind was still reeling from it, replaying the scene over and over. It had all happened so quickly.

By the time the ranch hands and he had heard the commotion and seen the bull, it was already happening. They did all they could to get the bull away from him. Josh tried desperately to get to the fence and roll under it to safety. However, with the bull's first strike, the animal had run his horn deep into Josh's side.

Deacon looked back from his seat on the helicopter, watching the two men dressed in white and splattered with his brother's blood working diligently on Josh. His own body was covered in blood, more blood than he imagined one person could have. Josh was in and out of consciousness, calling Deedra's name repeatedly in the delirium of pain. At times, Josh's body would thrash about, trying to free himself from the grasp of the men working on him or possibly still fighting off the bull's attack; he did not know. All Deacon could think to do was try to calm him with the sound of his voice.

"Hang in there, man, hang on, Josh! We're almost there! Just hang on, Josh! *Dear God, hang on. You have to be all right. You have to be!"*

They had paced and waited for two hours trying to get information on Josh. The nurses kept saying the same thing repeatedly. "We don't have any information yet." Deacon tried unsuccessfully several times to strong-arm the nurses by raising his voice and demanding attention so that he and Deedra could go back and be with him. Finally, after two and a half hours, the doctor came out to the waiting room to get Deedra. By now, Deedra was in full-swing panic, terrified, speculating what was happening with her husband.

Therefore, she was very grateful that they had come to take her back to be with him for a moment and let her know his condition. Lucy left an hour before to get Katy; Deacon hoped that by the time she arrived they would have some news to tell about her son.

The doctor stopped just outside Josh's room, realizing he had not yet introduced himself.

"I'm so sorry, Mrs. McKenzie, my name is Doctor Farley. I am one of the doctors called in on your husband's case."

Deedra nodded. This was no time for formalities. The only thing she cared about was having this man tell her what was going on.

"Your husband is in critical condition," the doctor continued, speaking matter-of-factly. "He has lost a lot of blood, his liver has been perforated, and we believe that his stomach may be as well. We are readying a surgical suite for him and will be taking him upstairs soon. In the meantime, we have been stabilizing him to send him through a CAT scan, to see the damage to his organs and bone structure. Once we have the required information, we will proceed with surgery to repair the damage. Do you have any questions at this time?"

"Will he be all right?" she stammered, trying to get the words out. She was frightened to hear the answer.

"I wish I had those answers, Mrs. McKenzie, but we won't know anything until we can see what damage there is to his body."

"I want to be with him; let me stay with him. I know he needs me."

"I'm afraid that's not possible. But, you can sit with him until they come down to get him. Once the surgery is complete, either I or one of my associates will be down to speak with you in the surgical waiting area."

"Just let me see him." The tears were falling down her cheeks.

"Josh? Honey?" Deedra bent down close to his face, careful not to touch him for fear of hurting him. "I'm right here, honey, I'm here with you," she whispered, fighting back the sobs, doing her best to keep her voice calm.

She still did not know the extent of his injuries. Deedra heard the doctor say that he had been given blood, something about liquids they were giving him in the I.V in his arm, and that they had worked diligently to stabilize him enough for surgery.

All she could comprehend is what she saw with her eyes. Lying on the gurney, both his body and sheet soaked with his blood, the once dark tanned face was pale. His beautiful mauve-colored lips were now a pasty gray color. Lifting the sheet carefully, she saw the deep bruises to his arms and neck. The tears streamed silently down her cheeks at the sight of how bad he looked. Quietly she eased herself down on the edge of the chair, scooting it close to him. She was deeply afraid for him to leave and go to surgery, afraid this would be the last time she would feel his warm body.

"Josh, can you hear me? Honey? I love you, love you so much. I'm so scared. Please, honey, you can't leave me, tell me you're going to be OK! Tell me you won't leave..." She wept.

The nurses ushered her out of the room, as they were ready to take him to the surgical unit. She bent down, softly kissing the bruised cheekbone. She whispered low against his ear, "Please come back to me, Josh, I can't do this without you. Please, Josh—fight with everything you have."

Standing just outside the door, watching them take him away, the tears fell hard, the sobbing grew loud. She was more frightened than she had ever been in her life. Deacon heard her sobs and promptly came to her aid, only to find Deedra leaning with her back to the wall, bent with her hands cupped over her face, sobbing uncontrollably. Grabbing her to him, he hugged her tightly, letting the tears fall against his shirt. Carefully he guided her to the waiting room and helped her to sit in one of the chairs there.

Deacon knew what Deedra had seen in the hospital room even without asking her. He was there, saw him covered in blood. He was petrified that he would not make it. He saw the bruising and swelling to his face and neck area, could see the blood oozing from his side. It was a gruesome site. It made him realize just how much he loved his brother, how much he meant to him.

"What went wrong, Deacon?" Deedra pleaded, looking up at him with sorrowful eyes, waiting for an answer. "Tell me what went wrong, why he's here?"

"Gawd, Deedra, he's been around those bulls for years," Deacon began, trying his best to tell her everything he could remember. "We were in the cow pens, had a bunch we were working. Something happened, I do not know what. I just…just heard this loud thud sound, and I turned and saw Josh going down. I heard Pete scream out. Some of the other hands were trying to get Josh away from that Brahma bull, you know the one we call Lonesome. Anyway, damn, he tried to get under the fence, roll under it, I mean. But, the bull made contact again." Deacon fell silent for a moment recalling the horrible events.

"I got the rifle off my horse. I shot him, shot Lonesome. I wasn't thinking, guess I didn't care, killed our prize bull. But, what could I do? He'd never acted like that before. I stayed with Josh, right on the ground, holding him." The tears were slowly streaming down his worried face; his words sounded more like someone rambling than actually making clear sentences. "Somebody called for an ambulance, I don't know. They sent a helicopter. I sent Pete to go get Lucy; she had to get you to the hospital."

"Oh my God, Deacon! He's going to be all right, isn't he?"

Deacon didn't answer the question; he didn't have the answer. Not answering only made Deedra's tears flow more freely, the feeling of fear more prominent.

Josh's mother and Lucy were sitting across from them, and they heard Deacon tell Deedra what happened. Both women were quietly praying.

For over seven hours they sat, prayed, and paced the floors. Deedra became more worried as each hour passed. She called Marcy, who was staying with the children. Marcy was not only being updated, but she was also trying to keep her dear friend from losing control.

Deacon and Lucy, impatiently waiting as well, hoped to hear some good news when the doctors were finished. In spite of the worry for Josh, they were also concerned for Deedra. They watched her sit for a few minutes, then begin pacing repeatedly. They could see she was becoming worn out and drained.

All Deedra could do was reflect. Her worst nightmare was coming true before her eyes. The feelings were reemerging, the dread of what would happen by marrying Josh. She knew they should not have wed, she had tried to tell him she was not good for him. She was a jinx, and she had brought a curse by marrying him. First her parents, then Craig and now Josh was hanging on to life by a thread.

The feeling of flight abruptly hit deep in her soul. The rage beat hard in her heart. She needed to run, pretend this was a bad dream, and go back to the safest place she knew—hiding within herself.

Right now, at this moment, she wanted to run and never look back. She could not imagine the loss of Josh, not now. This was a cruel trick being played on her. The pain of loss loomed over her like a sinister black cloud. Maybe if she left right now, Josh would be all right. The evil would lift itself from him.

I hate this, I hate myself. I knew better! I knew! This is all my fault. I should never have married him, I knew this would happen. I'm not meant to have happiness. I told him, tried to warn him. Damn it, Josh, I tried to tell you! The anger filled up like water in Deedra's heart.

She looked around the room, wondered if she could sneak away. Run home, get the children, leave this place and move far from here. Maybe Josh would be all right then. Maybe he would survive. In time he would forget about her, forget about her existence…

Deedra took hold of herself; finally, it dawned on her what she was thinking of doing. Saying these things, thinking these things was the same as showing disrespect for the man that loved her with all of his heart. How could she ever walk away from him, hurt him like that? Would he turn and run if something happened to her? No, no he wouldn't!

This time she would not allow herself to go back to the old Deedra, to run like a child from the pain. Josh had instructed her to listen and learn, love and allow to be loved. He taught her about resilience, strength, and freedom. It was on her shoulders now to prove to him that she was stronger than the woman she once was. She needed to prove that his teachings were not in vain.

There would be no walking away, nowhere to run or hide. She

would will Josh to live, she would not allow her mind to think for one moment that she might lose him. Josh had to survive this. He was her world, her existence, and her soul. They were going to be adding to their family soon. He would never leave her now, not now—not ever!

Looking up, Deedra caught a glimpse of a doctor in a long white coat out of the corner of her eye. Hurriedly, she wiped the tears from her eyes with her hands and then stood up to see if this doctor had news regarding Josh. In seconds, he was standing face to face with her. Her heart pounded wildly. She was unsure of the look on the doctor's face.

"Mrs. McKenzie?"

"Yes!" she confirmed nervously.

The doctor motioned for Deedra to sit because of her advanced pregnancy. Deacon, Lucy and the elder Mrs. McKenzie took a seat next to them.

"My name is Dr. Sinclair," he began. "I was called in on your husband's case, I'm one of several doctors that has been working on your husband. He has some extensive injuries, I'm afraid."

Deedra's sob could be heard outside of the room from the sound of that. *He has some extensive injuries, I'm afraid.* The doctor calmed her then continued.

"Mr. McKenzie's stomach was punctured, there was a lot of internal bleeding, but we were able to repair the damage and the bleeding is under control. His liver was perforated as well, and we have done everything possible to repair the damage, but he lost approximately twenty-five percent of the liver. His right hip was broken in several places, causing extensive damage. We repaired what we could and then fused a piece of his spine into the hip for support. He will have to have extensive therapy for the hip, which I will explain as we go along in his recovery. He has shattered his knee and we have replaced it as well, again he will need therapy. His forearm was broken, though not severely. He will be in a cast for about six to eight weeks for this to heal. Additionally, he has a concussion. This is our main concern for now, and it is causing some problems. We are watching him closely. At present, he is in a coma. We aren't sure how long this might last, but we are monitoring him closely and will re-run MRIs to watch for any brain swelling. He had a deep puncture wound from the bull's horn to his right side; this broke two of his ribs and caused the internal damage to the stomach and liver.

"I will tell you, Mrs. McKenzie, it is a good thing that he is a strong man. He is extremely lucky to have survived long enough for us to operate. Even more so, that he has remained stable and his body was able to withstand such extensive work to repair all of the damage."

"Will he be all right now?" Deedra interrupted, having sat so quietly listening.

"I wish I could tell you yes. Nevertheless, Mrs. McKenzie, the fact is, his body has been through a lot, and we have done everything we could possibly do. He has lost a lot of blood; there has been a lot of trauma. However, I will say it is remarkable that he has come this far, and his chances for survival will increase each hour, with the next forty-eight hours being the most crucial."

Deedra felt as though she might faint. The room seemed to be closing in around her, making it difficult to for her to breath. She stayed sitting on the chair, afraid to move for what might happen. The fears she had about losing him stared her in the face. They were trying their best to make her lose control again. She could not allow the thoughts to take over, could not allow anything to happen to Josh. She could never let him go.

"I have to go," she announced to the small worried crowd. With shaking legs and trembling hands, she went downstairs in the elevator as quickly as she could to find the small hospital chapel. Once there, she pleaded with God to spare Josh's life, begging that he not be taken away from her, adamant that He must spare his life.

He had to stay alive for their unborn baby, for the children sitting at home waiting for good news. He had to remain strong and firm. He had to be there to share in the joy of the first touch, the first kiss of their child. He could not die. She could not live through the death of this man. Their love was too magical, too strong, and too passionate to be ended like this.

Chapter 25

Numerous hours passed with many strong heartbeats felt pounding in Deedra's chest. Attentively she sat next to Josh's bed in the ICU unit, praying constantly. She begged God to give him strength. Each hour that ticked by, every precious moment of breath his body took was one more moment of life, one second closer to the 48-hour mark.

The intensive care unit was quiet and solemn. The different families coped with the tragedies together. The white walls, white tiles and burgundy-colored chairs made the room look plain and antiseptic. The waiting room for the respectful families had plain white walls, burgundy chairs and white tiles floors. There was nothing happy about the colors or decorations of the place, a place where families waited impatiently and each pleaded with a higher power to spare their loved one.

The family would take turns sitting with Josh, trying to allow Deedra hourly breaks. She did not want him to be alone for one second. Marcy had come to Deedra's aid as soon as she had gotten the word. She called Brad, and together they went to the ranch to care for the children as soon as the bus left them off from school. They would do their best to explain the situation and try to keep things calm for them.

Though Josh could not hear the words of encouragement Deedra whispered, or the prayers she spoke sitting next to him in the hard-backed chair, she believed he could and that she was willing him to live. Gently she would touch the areas of his body not destroyed by the bull, cooing her love for him, stroke his long, mangled, mess of hair.

Every few hours she would call Marcy and check on the children, then report anything she knew. She wished she had better news to tell for the children's sake. She was so tired, and so exhausted. So worried. Patiently she waited for a small sign that he was coming out of it. She read aloud to him from one of the magazines she found downstairs in the hospital's coffee shop.

Deacon sat down next to Deedra during one of her short breaks. He watched in admiration as her hands encircled her large stomach, trying to ease the ache of the baby's kicks.

"Kickin' much?" he asked.

"Oh yes." She smiled slightly.

"He's a little spitfire like his daddy, huh?" he said, trying to ease the situation slightly. "Has Josh said if he wants a boy or girl?"

"He's never said," she replied, still rubbing.

Deacon reached for her hand and put it in his. "It's gonna be all right, Deedra, my brother's a fighter." He was trying his best to reassure her.

Deedra glanced over to Katy. His mother hadn't left the hospital since she had arrived. She just sat quietly, silently praying. While Deedra took her break, Lucy sat with Josh.

Deedra thought to herself, *How afraid she has to be, that's her baby in there.* "Mrs. McKenzie, you need anything?" Deedra asked.

"No, nothing, but thank you."

"Are you doing OK?" she questioned.

"Doin' as good as I can," she responded. "I'm worried about you some, with the baby and all, you're wearing yourself out."

"Oh, I'm OK, Miss Katy, I'm OK."

"Call me Mom, Deedra, or Momma like my Josh does, OK?"

"I would love to…Momma." Deedra smiled faintly.

"You have Deacon take you down and get some good food in you! Not just coffee either, take some time and eat something." Katy made a motion with her hand for Deacon to get up from the chair.

"I will in a little bit," Deedra responded.

"No, you'll go now! I'll be here if anything happens," she ordered. Deacon stood up and grabbed for Deedra's hand, helping to lift her up. When they turned to walk away, Deedra heard him whisper, "You'll learn ya can't argue with Momma."

Deedra didn't realize how hungry she was. Deacon ordered soup, salad and a half a sandwich for her and she cleaned it up to the crumbs. While she ate, she and Deacon had a chance to talk a bit more, giving her the chance to know him on a different level. He wasn't that much different from Josh. A little harder maybe regarding some things, but basically he was the same type of man—boisterous, so sure of himself, demanding.

Deacon was able to see what his brother saw in Deedra as well. She was a fiercely devoted, loyal and honest woman. She was not overly beautiful, at least not in his eyes. But, Deacon could see the attractiveness of her. The wild curls of hair, the peach-soft skin and the large expressive eyes. It was those eyes that told him how much she loved his brother, the eyes and facial expressions she made when speaking of him. His brother had been truly blessed this time.

Deedra was not even remotely like the ex-wife, the leach— Lindsey. Though Lindsey thought she was a woman of money, she never carried it off very well. She had always looked more like a painted-up trollop than a decent woman. She had always tried her best to look sexy, yet never could quite pull it off. She spoke in a drawn-out, fake Georgian accent that she emphasized, with more vulgarities than both he and Josh put together could speak. She would spend Josh's money freely as if there were no tomorrow, and she had never tried to be family oriented, no matter what the event. *Hell, she wasn't even much of a mother.* Deacon had wondered many times why Josh would marry someone like her. But he had been extremely grateful when she decided to leave Josh and the boys behind to move on to greener pastures.

Deedra didn't seem to be anything like that. She always seemed to be pure and simple, elegant even in a t-shirt and pair of faded jeans. She fit Josh perfectly. Her softer side intermixed with his hard edges so well that they seemed to complement each other.

Deacon was thrilled by her and what she brought to his brother's life. He also liked this one-on-one conversation he was having with her, even though it was under these circumstances. He knew she made Josh happy. That's what mattered most of all to Deacon, though he'd be damned to ever say such things to Josh for fear of him thinking he was mushy.

Chapter 26

Josh's body jolted a little when the nurse touched his arms to check his vitals. This was the first major movement he had made in over fifty-five hours. *Has to be a good sign,* Lucy reasoned, running from the room to find Deedra.

By the time Deedra got to his bedside, Josh was softly moaning. In a state of high excitement over the fact that he seemed to be coming out of the coma, she moved the chair closer to the bed. Like a hawk she watched every tiny movement he made, holding tightly to his hand in hopes of feeling the fingers move. He was desperately trying to regain consciousness. Delicately, she kissed at his swollen and bruised lips, begging him to come back to her.

Persistently she talked to him, waiting, watching, begging him to fight to live. Finally, after two hours of patiently sitting, she saw his eyes slowly begin to flicker open and close. The moans became a little more pronounced. He was coming out of the coma, coming back to her.

"Josh? Can you hear me?" she whispered close to his ear. "Open your eyes, baby, come on! Come on, honey, you can do it." Still there was only the flicker of his eyes with no verbal response. Desperately, she tried to reach into his unconscious mind with her words. "Josh? Honey, please!" Again, she waited, hoping.

Standing just outside the hospital room door, Katy, Deacon and Lucy waited for confirmation. Deedra slouched back in the chair, dismayed by the fact that he still had not responded. The silent tears dripped off her chin. Deacon came to her side and bent down next to her chair and grabbed her tightly in a hug. Deedra let the anguished-filled tears flow. His own tears trickled as well.

Several more hours passed. They kept taking turns, softly talking to him in whispered voices. The prayers continued, the worried phone calls would come in to the nurse's station from family, and the time would pass. Every few hours, Deedra would call Marcy to update her and check on the children. She knew as hard as this was for her, it was equally as hard for the children, although they were young enough that they probably didn't understand everything that was going on.

Deedra went down to the small hospital shop located on the first floor and bought several books, figuring that if Josh couldn't respond for now, she would read to him. At least it would keep her mind busy.

After returning to Josh's room, she quietly positioned herself in the chair close to him.

"Deedra?" She faintly heard her name.

Her heart quickened. "Josh? Oh my God, Josh!" She saw his eyes flickering open and shut again. "Come on, Josh! I'm right here. Oh, honey, open your eyes. Look, I'm right here! Come on, come back to me. Please!"

His eyes cracked open, trying to focus, unable to see her for the swelling around his cheekbones and eyes. He was not able to remember what had happened or where he was.

"Deedra?" he called out again, the sound of fear in his voice.

"I'm right here, baby! Right here," she replied, smiling.

"Where...Where am I?" he weakly asked.

"The hospital, Josh. Oh God, I love you!" She bent closer to kiss his lips, whispering to him.

"Why? What's happened?

"You had an accident, honey."

"Why am I here?" He moaned, not understanding her answer.

"You had an accident. But everything's going to be all right now. You're going to be fine."

"Where am I?" he asked again, still not comprehending, trying to move his body away from the restraints surrounding him.

"You were hurt, honey. By a bull, do you remember?"

"No, I don't think so. God I hurt," he muttered.

"I know you do, honey. I know, I'm here for you." She shed tears for him.

"Don't leave me," he pleaded.

"No, no, I won't. I'm right here, honey."

Bit by bit, throughout the remaining evening she explained to him all that had happened to him over the last three days, trying to help him understand why he was in so much pain. When he spoke the words, "I love you," her heart sang out with an overabundance of joy. These were possibly the greatest words she could have ever heard.

Josh tried his best to stay determined, trying to deal with the constant pain. Even with all the medications, it hurt to move. It did not help matters any that he hated the confinements of the uncomfortable hospital bed.

All of his life he had lived in the country with fresh air and wide open spaces, and now he was cooped up in a small room that was so pragmatic and devoid of color, attached to several different monitors, with tubes running in his sides to allow for drainage, needles delivering fluids in his arm, and totally bedridden.

He was, however, thankful for the time Deedra stayed by his side. He was selfish to the point that he hated her to leave his side for a moment. She was what was making him well, helping him to endure the long days trying to heal. There were times he would beg her to go home, knowing she needed the rest and that she had to take better care of herself. However, when she would go the walls would close in and he would get upset and angry with himself for letting her go.

He took his frustrations out on the staff, because the rock that held him together was not there to keep his anger at bay. Every day that she could be with him, she would. She read to him and talked to him about what was going on around him and at the ranch. She made the pain so much easier to bear.

She was there through the convalescence and every long therapy session, willing him on. Every day, she was by his side, pushing him to overcome the obstacles. Lovingly, she would bathe him and wash his hair, then brush it out to dry. She caressed his arms as they healed. She read to him until he would fall asleep, then ease back in her own makeshift cot the hospital had given her to get some rest as well. Deedra would keep the bold and boisterous man from becoming depressed over the situation he was living with.

With the help of the medication, Josh slept through the night like a baby, while Deedra, uncomfortable from her bulky frame, would toss and turn. As much as she wanted to, it was just too hard staying every night. No matter what, though, she spent every moment she could with him. Regrettably, every few days Josh would lose his temper. Deedra would calm him by whispering to him and stroking his long hair.

Many weeks were spent in the hospital. They were long, agonizing days for Josh, as he was going through the painfully rigorous therapy sessions. Being there for him as much as she was, Deedra had missed several doctor's appointments. She had also canceled the ultrasound. There was no way she wanted to find out the sex of the baby without Josh. They argued about it, but she told him directly that the ultrasound would wait until he was there to share it with her.

Except this morning, she wished she had gone to the doctor's office. Her stomach was enormous and extremely uncomfortable. Her back throbbed constantly and her energy level was almost zilch. She was exhausted from the trips back and forth trying to care for Josh, and the long trips home to see about the children. It was wearing her down, causing her stomach to twinge relentlessly. Though her back hurt even more than usual, and she was experiencing mild cramping, she thought there was nothing she could not handle. Deedra would not complain for fear of worrying Josh.

"Good morning, honey," she cooed, watching her man move his body, trying to stretch the muscles after its long sleep.

"Good morning to you too, did you sleep OK?" He beamed, delighted to see her.

"I slept fine." She grinned, telling him a fib.

Suddenly a cramp hit her. Deedra sat there for a moment, trying to relax herself and keep from alerting Josh in any way.

"Wanna take a walk with me after breakfast, Sunshine?" Josh

asked, proud of himself that he could walk for very short distances with the help of a cane.

"That sounds good. I had better go on down to the cafeteria and have my breakfast. You should have yours soon, so when I get back we will go on that walk."

Another cramp hit and she grimaced a little, and then waited for the cramp to ease so she could lift her large frame from the chair. Carefully, she leaned over to kiss him.

"I'll be back shortly." She smiled sweetly, then turned toward the door.

"Hey, Deedra!" Josh called out to her. "I love you."

Turning back to him, she smiled again, then put her fingers to her lips in a kissing fashion and blew the kiss out to him.

Fresh hot coffee and a huge Danish looked mighty good this morning. She sat down carefully to enjoy it, complaining to herself yet again how much her back really ached today. Another cramp came upon her. Involuntarily, she reached for her stomach on that one; it was much harder than any of the prior ones.

"OK, little one, settle down now," she spoke to herself, massaging the large bulging stomach. "You better calm it down, you're really hurting Mommy. You still have a few weeks yet, so behave!"

"You ready for that walk, Mr. McKenzie?" she announced, sauntering into the room.

"I sure am, Mrs. McKenzie." He laughed. "You sure you're up to walking?" he questioned, a worried look on his brow. "You're awfully pale, didn't you eat?"

"Oh, I'm fine! In fact I probably ate too much," she explained, not quite telling the truth.

This time when another cramp hit, she was practically unable to hide it from him. She took in a deep breath and regrouped herself enough to start their walk. *These have to be Braxton-Hicks contractions*, she reflected, speculating what it really might be. After all, she had nearly four weeks left until her due date. Josh would be doing so much better then.

Rounding the corner on the last leg of their walk, another cramp hit and stopped her cold in her tracks. She could not hide this one from Josh.

"Deedra? What's wrong?" he inquired, a bit troubled by the look on her face.

"Just having those stupid false contractions, I guess," she reasoned, perplexed by the contractions herself.

"You sure 'bout that?" he questioned again.

"Yeah, they will go away; the baby just wants attention I think." Josh cut his eyes at her, a puzzled look on his face.

"Really, Josh, I'm fine, now don't start worrying."

They were not quite to the room when another cramp hit, this one harder than all the others. In synchronization with the cramp, her water broke and came gushing to the floor.

"Oh my God!" Josh yelled. "Somebody get a wheelchair! It's my wife," he screamed and then reached for Deedra's hand to steady her. One of the nurses, Betty, came running toward them. Josh steadily yelled back for her to stop and get him some help.

"Her water broke, you need to get her help," he yelled at the nurse.

Deedra was not saying a word, she was too busy holding tightly to her stomach, astonished that this was happening now. *Not now! Not with everything else.*

"When did this start?" Betty queried.

"I've been having twinges, nothing major, most of the morning."

One of the supervisors on Josh's floor came running as well, bringing a wheelchair with her. "Let's get you upstairs to the OB Unit," the supervisor stated, helping her into the chair.

"I'm going with her!" Josh demanded.

"Sir, I'm sorry, but you can't go, you're under our care," the nurse stated.

"Bet me, I said I'm going! That's my baby she's having!" Josh argued back in a loud tone.

"OK, Mr. McKenzie! But you ride in a wheelchair if you do, you're not to be walking that much yet," she snapped back.

"Oh, for Gawd Sakes, woman," he said, rolling his eyes at her.

"Wheelchair or you don't go," the supervisor demanded.

"Get the damn wheelchair then! Good Gawd, can't you see she needs help? All you're worried about is a damn chair! Well, haven't you got the chair yet?" Josh exclaimed excitedly, giving a hard look at the nurse.

While the nurses on the OB floor settled Deedra into her room, hooking the monitors and starting an IV, Josh was nervously trying to remember numbers, calling everyone he could think of. He wasn't sure if any of them understood what he was saying over the phone or not. In typical Josh fashion, he was screaming at them to get there quickly.

"Get here, the baby is coming!" he yelled, panicked and shaking like a leaf. His nervousness was so evident that he was fidgeting with the different items in the room, looking through the cabinet doors, waiting to get close enough to speak to Deedra. Finally, with his patience on the brink of becoming explosive for not being able to get close to her for the nurses, he wheeled himself out to the hallway. Before he could take in a good long breath, Marcy was racing up the hallway.

"Damn, woman, did you fly?"

"You bet I did! What happened? Is she all right?" Marcy was popping out questions faster than Josh could begin to answer them.

"If you wait a minute I'll tell you," he remarked nervously. "Her water broke, that's what I know. She's in labor. Those idiots will not let me get close enough to find out nothing! Really pissin' me off about it too!" He was being cantankerous and hoping that if he complained loudly enough they would let him in just to shut him up.

"You know this is my fault! Gawd, Marcy, what have I done?"

"Josh, now don't say that! You know that's not true."

"I do know! I know she's been dealing with me and doing way too much. Damn it! She should have had a worry-free pregnancy, that's what I told her I wanted her to have. No stress!"

"Josh, you didn't ask to get hurt."

"Yeah, well." He went quiet, stewing in his own anger.

"Yeah well nothing! You could not help what happened," Marcy retorted.

"I promised her—"

Nothing Marcy said to calm him seemed to help. He believed wholeheartedly that because of the accident and the stress she was under, he had put her in this position.

I demanded too much attention from her, she was not able to care for herself the right way. Gawd I am so stupid, I knew she should have rested more. But no, I wanted her with me. Begged her to stay with me. What I should have been was a man and dealt with it like one instead of doing this to her.

By the time they finally let him in the room, he was beside himself with anxiety.

"Hey, Sunshine!" Josh greeted his wife, trying to lighten himself up a bit so she couldn't tell how anxious he was. She did not answer, as she was right in the middle of a hard contraction. If he was not worried enough, watching her in the middle of the contraction scared him to death.

"God, what's happening to her?" Josh questioned the nurse, fear in his eyes.

"She's in labor, Mr. McKenzie," the nurse responded.

"I'm not stupid, I know that! I've had two kids, but her pain shouldn't be this bad!"

"She's doing just fine, sir," the nurse answered, wanting to roll her eyes at the way he was talking to her, but deciding against it. He was just overly concerned.

"Josh?" Deedra whispered. "The nurse says we can't turn back! I'm dilating too quickly," she replied nervously.

"Well, where's the doctor then?"

"He's on his way, they called him." However, before she could say anything else another contraction hit.

"The doctor is on his way, Mrs. McKenzie, just keep breathing." The nurse spoke in a soothing tone, watching the needle that registered her contractions.

"He needs to get here now!" Josh ordered.

The nurse continued her words, not responding to his statement.

"Honey, come here," Deedra implored him.

Josh wheeled himself closer to the bed and Deedra grabbed for his hand.

"Look, honey, you have to calm down. It's not the nurses' fault. And it's doing nothing for you either, just try and calm down."

"I know, I know, I'm just worried about you." He apologized.

"I know, honey." She squeezed at his hand.

"Anyway, Marcy is just outside, she's worried about you."

For the next thirty minutes, Marcy helped Deedra use the breathing techniques to ease the contractions up a little. She rubbed her stomach gently during the contractions themselves. Josh, in the meantime, was growing weaker by the minute and wheeling his chair back and forth in a pacing motion in the room and up and down the halls. Finally, in anger over having to sit in the chair, he stood and pushed the chair over to the corner.

This is no time for me to be a pussy, sitting in that idiotic chair. Deedra needs me to stand up and be a man.

He would hobble over when a contraction hit and try to put his hands on her, even with the cast, and whisper softly to her. Silently, he was cursing the pain she was enduring, knowing how scared she was that the baby was coming too soon. He wished he could take the pain away.

After the contractions would end, he would stroke her sweat-dampened hair as best he could and give her ice chips to suck. Then he'd go back to his silent pacing until the next contraction hit. He was in so much pain from being up on his legs. His ribs ached, but he had to fight the pain to be there for Deedra.

"Well hello, Deedra," Dr. Rapin called to her, entering the room. The doctor pulled the curtain around in front of them, excluding Marcy and Josh. Dr. Rapin checked Deedra's cervix. It was almost completely softened. She was extremely close to the ten centimeters she needed to deliver. After the exam, he explained that even though she was early, they could not stop her contractions since her water had already broken. No matter what they might want, the baby wanted to come now. He reassured her that the baby was large even though she was early, and so he was very hopeful that the baby would be fine.

Josh tried to keep her reassured while she was trying her best to deal with the contractions. He knew she was scared to death as to what was going to happen; he was just as frightened for her and the baby. Panic filled both of their minds; what if something was wrong with the baby?

Leaning over the bed, Josh kissed Deedra's forehead. Silently he watched, stroking her as she finished the last of the contraction's pain. He turned to see his mother, Katy, walk through the door.

"I'm only allowed to stay a minute," she declared, walking toward the bed. "I had to give you something to keep." She opened her hand, depositing something into Deedra's hand. Deedra looked to see an exquisite antique-looking sterling silver locket and rope chain. Deedra was in awe of its intricate lace-like details.

"This was my grandma's necklace. She was wearing it the day my mama was born. When Grandma died she told my mama to give it to me, now I'm giving it to you."

"It's so beautiful, Momma. I couldn't possibly take this." A small tear rolled down her cheek.

"I have saved it for the right woman, Deedra. Now you keep it. You do what you want with it, it's yours. It will bring you luck today." Katy patted Deedra's shoulder with her hand, smiling. In turn, Deedra kissed Katy's hands and promised to care for it and hand it down as well.

The smile left her face, though, when the next contraction hit, harder than any of the others she had.

"I better go," Katy stated quickly. "I'll see you soon, Josh, I love you."

Josh was helpless sitting there watching as she went through the pain. His accident, the contractions, this new life inside of her that she carried. Deedra had been through so much; he hated her going through this too.

The nurses tried to give her something to ease the pain a little, but she refused, worried that any medication might do more harm than good for her baby. The baby was coming early as it was, she did not want to add to any problems the baby might have at birth.

"Josh," Deedra cried out softly during a hard contraction that seemed to rip her stomach wide open. "I'm so scared."

"I know, baby, I know, everything will be OK. It will be over soon, I promise," he said, trying to calm her.

"No! I mean something's wrong!" she yelled out. "The pain is too intense, something's wrong!"

"It's OK, baby." He smoothed her forehead and hair, then asked Marcy to go get the doctor.

Returning with the nurse in tow, they watched as she pulled back the sheets to see what was going on.

"Something's wrong!" Deedra cried out to the nurse, trying to get someone to understand her apprehension.

"It's all right, Mrs. McKenzie, the baby's head is just beginning to crown, that's all. Let's get you ready for delivery, OK?"

Josh watched while the nurse broke down the end of the bed, moving it away, and brought over the instruments on a table. *Now this is new, when Lindsey gave birth,* she *labored in one room and delivered in another. Now here we are in a room you do it all in,* he thought, watching with intent.

"It's going to be all right, honey, hang in there." Josh tried to have a soothing voice, but his own nervousness was shining through.

"No, Josh! Why will no one listen! Something's wrong, I can feel it!" The panic was heard clearly in the tone of her voice.

No matter what the nurse or the doctor tried to say, she still felt panicked. Deedra was overly agitated. The fear she was feeling was starting to play tricks on her, making her believe that the baby was in severe danger.

"Mrs. McKenzie, the baby is coming," the nurse spoke gently, trying to soothe her. "Try to calm yourself and continue your breathing exercises."

The labor-delivery room was a beautiful shade of blue with light hues of blue sprinkled throughout the room. For most, this would be a peaceful place to bring a child in to the world, but for Deedra there was no peace whatsoever.

Josh was asked to leave and get his scrubs on so that he could be in the room during the delivery. In just a few minutes, he was storming back into the room, afraid that if he had stayed a second longer, he would miss the delivery.

Standing beside his wife's bed, he tried his best to keep her as calm as possible. He felt as if he might faint, not from the birth, but from being up on his feet much longer than he should have been. He was feeling weaker by the minute, but swore under his breath that he would not let Deedra down.

The pains of contraction after contraction took hold of her body, ripping through it like a knife. Still, this could not be happening. She prayed hard to herself that the baby would be all right.

Dr. Rapin walked in, coming to the foot of the bed. "OK, Deedra…when I tell you to push, you push as hard as you can."

The pain hit like a ton of bricks against her stomach, the feeling of a white-hot flame going up her spine.

"Push, Deedra," Dr. Rapin ordered.

With each push, Deedra got a little closer and Josh became weaker and even more afraid.

"Next push, Deedra, I want you to look in the mirror, you'll see the baby's head," the doctor instructed.

"Push, Deedra, push hard!"

Josh looked down between Deedra's thighs to see the small patch of dark matted hair emerge slightly. "Oh Gawd, Deedra, I see the baby's head," he squealed, tears welling up in his eyes. "Push, Deedra, come on, I see the baby," Josh was yelling excitedly.

"Oh God!" Deedra screamed out. Then came another long scream and growl.

"Stop pushing, Deedra, hang on a minute," the doctor instructed.

Deedra lay there panting. The doctor turned the baby's head slightly so that the shoulders would come out.

"OK, Deedra, one last push!" The doctor held tightly to the baby's shoulder, helping it to enter into the world.

"It's a boy!" Dr. Rapin announced cheerfully.

"Oh my God, my son! I have another son!" Josh bent down, kissing Deedra repeatedly on her lips, so excited by the small black-haired little bundle.

"Is the baby OK?" Deedra questioned, and then didn't hear anyone answer. "Doctor, is the baby OK?"

"He's fine, a little small, but he's doing well."

"Oh," Deedra yelped loudly, her hand automatically reaching for the sharp pain in her stomach.

"What's happening? What's wrong?" Josh asked the doctor, a terrified look on his face as he tried to get back to Deedra's bed.

Dr. Rapin handed the baby to the nurse and examined Deedra to see what was wrong. "Well, looks like you're getting two for the price of one," Dr. Rapin announced to the stunned parents.

"What?" Josh yelled out, feeling a bit of shock. "How's that possible? There was only one heartbeat, Doc, remember?"

"Yes, well, your wife is delivering another baby, Mr. McKenzie."

Deedra had no words, her body thrust back into delivering again. Deedra let out a sharp scream with her push.

"Well, Deedra, my dear, this one's a little girl!" the doctor proclaimed proudly, overjoyed with himself for delivering twins.

"No more!" Deedra announced weakly. "No more in there I hope?"

It made Josh and the doctor both chuckle.

"That one sure hid from us, Deedra, we never picked up the extra heartbeat." Dr. Rabin was beaming. "She must have been behind her brother or something."

"Is she all right?" Deedra questioned.

"They're a little small, Deedra, like I said, but they're doing well. I do think they will have to stay in the incubator for a little bit."

They had prepared themselves a couple of months prior with the names for a boy or girl, never imagining in their wildest dreams that they would have twins. Tyler Joshua had been picked for a boy and Diana Elizabeth for the girl's name. Now, with two babies lying in the incubator, the names just did not seem to fit.

"Deedra, let me name them, please," Josh whispered.

Deedra nodded, too tired to speak now.

Josh touched the tiny infant's hand lying in the incubator next to her brother, both of them being cleaned by the nurses.

"When can I hold them?" Deedra questioned.

"Not just yet, Mrs. McKenzie," a nurse spoke up out of the distance of her sight. "We need to clean them up, and because of their birth weight, we want to keep an eye on them, so they will be in the incubator to make sure that everything will be OK."

"But they are OK, aren't they?" Deedra worried.

"Yes, I think they will be just fine," the nurse answered back.

"They will be, won't they?" Josh asked, looking up from the babies and into the nurse's eyes, making sure she was telling the truth.

"Yes, I believe they will, it's a precaution we take whenever a baby is born small," she replied.

"Josh," Deedra called out to him. "Let's not give them same name stuff like most twins have, OK? I want their names to be unique, you know, individuals."

"Yeah, you're right, baby! What do you think about the name Stella Renee?" He smiled down at the dark-haired child, waiting for Deedra to answer, while looking at the little wisp of black thin hair a top her head, still touching the little fingers.

"I think its beautiful, Josh. Where did the name Stella come from?" she questioned.

"It was my grandmother's name," Josh answered, smiling.

"I'm thinking maybe John Tyler for our little man's name. What do you think about that?"

"I think it's strong like you, Josh, perfect!"

Josh touched the little black-haired wonder, whispering his name. "John."

John weighed in at a whopping 3 lbs and 7 oz. His sister Stella, though hidden from view in her mother's stomach, apparently had eaten better than her brother and weighed in at 4lbs and 1 oz. Both of the little bundles were exactly 18 inches long.

Deedra slept for most of the night from the exhaustion, waking only for minutes at a time to inquire about the babies and to make sure they were all right. Josh, in his wheel chair sitting outside the thick-glassed wall of the neo-natal unit, watched his babies breathe in and out. He was so worn out and weak, and he needed rest desperately, but he could not break himself away from the precious newborns.

Nurses came up from his floor to do his vitals and give him his medications, each looking in on the new arrivals and remarking about how beautiful they were. They tried several times to get Josh to go back to his room and get the rest he needed. He was not out of the woods completely himself, and was very pale and shaky. He would not hear of it. In his mind, his place was to be with his wife and babies. He still could not believe that he had twins. He was so ecstatic, so proud of them.

They both had their father's large expressive eyes and deep dark hair. John had the most hair on his head, with his sister Stella getting only a small dusting of the deep color. They were so pink, perfect and beautiful.

Their family was finally complete. Everything that Josh had wanted for most of his life was his now. A woman to love him, beautiful children to teach and watch grow. The perfect set of three boys and three girls. All he could have ever wanted in life was his.

Chapter 27

The Coming Months

The family had been ecstatic. No one could have ever imagined that this was the reason Deedra was so huge during the pregnancy. With all that Josh had been through, Deedra staying by his side throughout and missing her ultrasound, she had missed the opportunity to find out she was having twins.

Determined not to go home without her babies, Deedra spent every moment she could between sitting with them in the neo-natal unit and sitting with Josh. Every day she would spend time with the children then go down to cheer Josh through his physical therapy sessions. Every night, they would lovingly watch through the window at the two bundles of love they had created.

The nursing staff finally gave in and put the couple in a larger room with two beds. Now she could stay with Josh through the night and together they spent the day with the babies, watching them grow, listening for them to cry, wanting the chance to nurse.

Dr. Rapin and the new babies' pediatrician, Dr. Shannon, were absolutely thrilled that though they were born with a small birth weight, everything else about them seemed perfectly normal. As long as they continued to grow as they were doing, Dr. Shannon saw no reason why they could not go home when they reached a weight of 5 lbs.

Josh would beam with pride when he would walk into the neo-natal unit and see Deedra nursing the small wonders. God, it was a beautiful picture.

"Well hi there, Daddy!" she called out to him, making him beam even greater with an overabundance of pride.

"I have a surprise for you," Josh sang out.

"You do, what is it?" she inquired.

"Well, ya know the whole group has been goin' nuts wanting to see you and the twins. So, I worked it out and got them all up here to visit for a few minutes."

"Oh, that's great! Well, get them in here!" she squealed.

Josh left the room and in a matter of minutes was back parading the group and introducing each baby to its new sister, brother, aunt or uncle. So much pride radiated from his heart. Each person was given the chance to hold each baby, coo, and kiss the little soft bundles.

While everyone else was deep in the moment, enjoying the small newborns, Deedra sat quietly in the rocking chair, saying a silent prayer. She was so thankful to the powers that be for bringing Josh in to her life, for him having the fortitude to fight for and with her so that they could be together, and for sparing him from the terrible accident. Except for the hip, which he still had many problems with and would have for the rest of his life, he was going to make a full recovery. His liver was regenerating itself. The stomach lining had healed nicely. The x-rays showed that each broken bone was healing well, with the exception of his hip and some minor remaining damage to the knee. The doctors had done everything they could to repair the damage too, but the injury would permanently leave Josh with a pronounced limp when he walked. The knee would not get any stronger than it was either. So, between the two, he would have some lingering pain in those areas. It was a small price to pay, though, for what could have happened to him.

Deedra was grateful for the new babies as well, pleased that though born small, they were growing at rapid speed and would go home soon. She was thankful for the new lives they would all begin when they got home.

Neither could hardly wait. Josh would be released soon, with Deedra and the babies following behind just two weeks later. The lives of the McKenzies would return to a more normal existence, with love that would fill the house with their extended family. This large family would be more than Deedra could ever have imagined would happen for her in this lifetime.

For the first time in her life, she was comfortable in her skin. A true feeling of honor radiated in her heart that she was the wife of a rancher, a true cowboy like her father had been. Never again would she be ashamed of her birthright or, for that matter, that of her husband's.

Together, they found an undying love, and in that love they had created a magic that would cross the barriers for generations to come. Just as Buck and Katy had accomplished in leaving behind memories of hard work, love, and laughter, Josh and Deedra would do the same for their children. One day, many years from now, she imagined there would be someone coming into one of their children's lives, and the child would retell the stories like Josh had relayed to her regarding how the ranch came to be. There would be the same pride in their eyes when they told them. The McKenzie name would live on into infinity.

The only sound heard within the walls of the large living room was the crackling of the wood burning in the fireplace. There was a sense of wonder in the air, of peace. The faint scent of baby powder lingered from the last changing of the twins.

They were home. The visitors had come and gone throughout the past two and a half weeks, making for a hectic schedule. Friends and family were doing their best to help Deedra and Josh make the transition home, reorganize the house to include the newborn twins, and help them settle back in to their home and lives.

It seemed such a long time ago that Deedra was scared of the world. Long gone was the cold and bitter heart she held so dearly. Also gone was the devastating accident Josh endured. It was more like a bad dream they had woken from, than actually something they had endured. Though Josh had a pronounced limp, somehow it made him even sexier than before, more manly.

In the quiet of this peaceful night, Deedra reflected on the events that had transpired in such a short period of time. The mysterious beauty of a special love had found its way with Fate's guidance through the difficult beginnings.

Then she realized something else while sitting there. In her relaxed state, her mind went free. The visions of her years as a teenager came flooding through her mind. Not the bad memories, but the sweet memories shared with Marcy at one of the sleepovers at her house.

The vision was of her as a sixteen-year-old, conveying a dream she had experienced the night before. She was remembering the memory of a man that was in this dream. Marcy had listened intently, enjoying her every recollection. She told Marcy this man was her "fantasy man." Deedra forced herself to concentrate harder on the image of this man, trying to bring him to the forefront of her mind. She saw his face as clear as though it were yesterday. It was Josh's face. The same tall, strongly built, dark-haired, dark-skinned man she had dreamt of so many years before.

Oh My God! It dawned on her. *He was the fantasy man! That is why I thought I knew him the first time I saw him at the restaurant. I was so sure we had met somewhere before, but I couldn't place him. He was always there in the back of my mind! He was not a teenager's dream after all, he was my reality, my destiny. It is why the scent of him was in my bedroom, even though he had never even been in my house. It is why I was so drawn to him, even when I thought I despised him. He was always there! He was not my teenage fantasy. I was actually looking into my future!*

"What you thinking about?" Josh asked, sitting down on the couch next to her.

He startled her for a moment with his voice, almost telling him her thoughts. At the last minute she decided no one would ever believe her epiphany, so she would just keep it to herself.

"Peacefulness, I think," she answered, patting his leg. "Just listen to it."

Leaning back against the couch, he closed his eyes and listened, hearing only the crackle of fire. "Yep, baby, this is nice, huh?" Then he pulled her over to him, hugging her tightly, and breathed in the delicate fragrance of her hair.

"Josh? I've been thinking."

"About?"

"Contacting my brother and sister. I mean, contacting Mark and Leslie. I think they should know about the twins, about my life."

"That would be wonderful, Sunshine. What made you decide?"

"I don't know, I guess maybe starting anew. Maybe because of what we have been through?"

"Whatever your reasons, I'm behind you! Whatever you decide."

"I love you so much, Josh!" She smiled.

"Now, you wanna guess what I'm thinking?" Josh asked sheepishly.

"Hmm, let me think a minute," she said, putting her finger to her temple, then closing her eyes as if she were using psychic powers to find the answer. "No, can't see it. Guess I don't have ESP." She laughed aloud.

He poked at her ribs, and she laughed even louder.

"You sure you don't know?" He smiled coyly, enjoying her laughter.

"Hmm, no sir, sorry, nothing comes to mind." She shrugged playfully.

"I'm thinking I want to make mad passionate all-night-long love to you! Right here, right now!" He grinned widely. "You think you're up for it?"

"Oh, Josh, I was up for it...oh, about a week or so ago!"

"Then why didn't you tell me?"

"Well, 'cause our lives were just a little hectic, I thought we needed some time to get everything settled a bit, you know, back to normal. If there is such a thing."

"I know I love you, Sunshine."

"I know I love you too."

Together they turned out all the lights downstairs, then retreated to their upstairs bedroom with its own crackling fireplace. Josh took a quilt from the closet and laid it out on the floor in front of the fire.

It had been so long since they had been able to be together, their lives had been altered by the accident and then the subsequent births of the babies.

The wait would be worth it, this night. They would come together in a fiery, passion-filled embrace, lying on the large feather-filled quilt. The hunger they had for each other would reignite the need that had been put on hold for so long. It was a need that was filled with burning desire and begging to be quenched. They welcomed the sweltering, destined love that would fill up their senses and renew their spirits.

Long departed from their lives forever more was the ice that had so tightly bound itself around Deedra's soul, the ghost of the past had been laid to rest, along with the bitterness and anger. Josh's own deep-seated resentments were now only a distant remembrance of his past as well. The apprehensions and past disappointments were nothing more than shadowed memories, as though a part of someone else's existence.

All that would remain would be the overwhelming passion and unforgettable phenomenon they had been fortunate enough to find within each other's hearts.

Printed in the United States
40260LVS00002B/36